张爱玲

少帅

北京出版集团公司
北京十月文艺出版社

青马〔天津〕文化有限公司
出　品

前言

宋以朗

　　一九九七年，我的母亲邝文美为了方便学者研究张爱玲，将一批张爱玲遗稿的复印本捐给南加州大学的东方图书馆。这批遗稿成为了南加州大学"张爱玲资料特藏"的重要部分，当中包括未刊英文小说《少帅》的打字稿复印本。我现在家中还有大量张爱玲的书信和作品手稿，正考虑该如何处置。很多人认为应该捐给大学做学术用途，原则上我没有理由反对，但事实上宋家早在十七年前已经把大批手稿捐到学术机构了，可惜效果未如理想。以《少帅》为例，十多年就这样过去了，我依然没有见到任何学者的研究，将来很可能还是会无人问津，所以我决定把它出版。

　　《少帅》是张爱玲当年锐意打入美国市场之作，结果因为各种理由而没有完成。今天张爱玲的读者始终是看中文的居多，所以我按照《雷峰塔》和《易经》的先例，找人把《少帅》翻译为中文。本书的中译者是郑远涛。

二○○九年出版《小团圆》，我为免众说纷纭，特地写了一篇前言交代张爱玲的创作前因后果。但出版前我没有想过，原来很多人是看不懂《小团圆》的写作手法的。他们看不出"穿插藏闪"的结构，竟以为是杂乱无章的草稿，令我非常诧异。汲取了那次经验，我找冯睎乾为《少帅》写了一篇考证和评析的文章，收录在别册里。那不是什么官方解读，只是我觉得尚算达标的研究，有兴趣的读者不妨参考一下。由于冯文会透露小说情节，读者切忌跳过小说翻阅这篇文章。

目　录

少帅

张爱玲 著　郑远涛 译

一

　　府里设宴，女孩子全都走出洋台看街景。街上有个男人把一只纸折的同心方胜儿掷了上来。她们拾起来拆开读道：

　　"小姐，明日此时等我。"

　　一群人蜂拥着跑回屋里。她们是最早的不缠足的一代，尽管穿着缎鞋，新式的"大脚"还是令她们看起来粗野嘈闹。

　　"肯定是给你的。"她们把纸条传来传去。

　　"瞎说，怕是给你的吧。"

　　"这么多人，怎么偏偏就我了？"

　　"谁叫你这么漂亮？"

　　"我漂亮？是你自己吧。我压根儿没看见是怎样的一个人。"

　　"谁又看见了？大家跑起来我还不知是为什么。"

　　周四小姐年纪太小，无须替自己分辩，只笑嘻嘻的，前刘海黑鸦鸦遮住上半张脸。她们留下来过夜。次日那钟点，女孩子们都说：

"去看看那人来了没有。"

她们躲在一个窗户后面张望，撅着臀部，圆鼓鼓的仿佛要胀破提花绸裤，粗辫子顺着乳沟垂下来。年纪小的打两根辫子，不过多数人是十八九岁，已经定了亲等过门。她们对这事这样兴冲冲的，可见从来没爱过。那种痴痴守望一个下午的情态，令四小姐有点替她们难为情。那男人始终没来。

她自己情窦早开。逢年过节或是有人过生日，她都会到帅府去。那里永远在办寿宴，不是老帅的便是某位姨太太的生辰，连着三天吃酒，请最红的名角儿登台唱堂会，但是从来不会是少爷们的生日，小辈庆生摆这种排场是粗俗的。总是请周家人"正日"赴宴，免得他们撞见军官一流的放诞之徒。帅府大少爷自己就是军官，有时穿长衫，有时着西装，但是四小姐最喜欢他一身军服。穿长衫被视为颓废，穿西装一副公子哥儿模样，再不然就像洋行买办。军服又摩登又爱国。兵士不一样，他们是荷枪的乞丐。老百姓怕兵，对军官却是敬畏。他们手握实权。要是碰巧还又年青又斯文，看上去就是国家唯一的指望了。大少爷众人都叫他"少帅"，相貌堂堂，笑的时候有一种嘲讽的神气，连对小孩子也是这样。他们围着他转。他逗他们开心，对着一只断了线的听筒讲个不停。四小姐笑得直不起身。有一回她去看唱戏的上装，有个演员借了少帅的书房做休息室，不过已经出场了。

"怎么你不剪头发？"少帅问，"留着这些辫子干吗？咱们现在是民国了。"

他拿着剪刀满房间追她，她笑个不停，最后他递来蓬松的黑色的一把东西，"喏，你想留着这个吗？"

她马上哭了。回去挨骂不算，还不知道爹会怎样讲。但原来只是一副髯口。

她在亲戚家看过许多堂会，自己家里的也有。不比散发霉味的戏园子，家里是在天井中搭棚，簇新的芦席铺顶，底下一片夏荫。刚搭的舞台浴在蓝白色的汽油灯光线下，四处笑语喧喧，一改平日的家庭气氛。她感到戏正演到精彩处而她却不甚明白，忍不住走到台前，努力要看真切些，设法突出自己，任由震耳的锣钹劈头劈脑打下来。她会两只手搁在台板上，仰面定定地瞪视。女主角站在她正上方咿咿呀呀唱着，得意洋洋地甩着白色水袖，贴面的黑片子上的珠花闪着蓝光。两块狭长的胭脂从眼皮一直抹到下巴，烘托出雪白的琼瑶鼻。武生的彩脸看上去异常阔大，像个妖魔的面具，唱腔也瓮声瓮气，仿佛是从陶面具底下发出声音。他一个腾空，灰尘飞扬，四小姐能闻到微微的马粪味。她还是若有所失。扶墙摸壁，绕行那三面的舞台。前排观众伸出手，护着摆在脚灯之间沏了茉莉香片的玻璃杯。在戏园里，她见过中途有些人离开包厢，被引到台上坐在为他们而设的一排椅子上。他们是携家眷姨太太看戏的显贵。大家批评这是粗俗的摆阔，她倒羡慕这些人能够上台入戏；尽管从演员背后并不见得能看到更多。

那时候她还小，还是大家口中的"吴蟠湖那会儿"。再之前是段庆莱时代。"现在是冯以祥了。""南边是方申荃。"军阀们的名字连老妈子都说得上来。她们也许不晓得谁是大总统，但是永远清楚哪个人实权在握，而且直呼其名。在一个名义上的共和国里，这是民主政治的唯一而奇特的现象。只是老帅因与本府老爷关系特殊，不在此例。哪个军阀起了倒了，四小姐印象模糊。审慎与自矜兼有的心理使他们家讳言战争，仿佛那不过是城市治安问题，只要看紧门户，不出去就行了。"外面正打着呢，谁也不许出去。"同时她听见远处的隆隆枪声。塾师如常授课，只是教女孩子们英文的英国女人暂时不来了。

"菲碧·周，一九二五年"——英文教师让她在自己每一本书的扉页上都写上这行字。"菲碧"只是为了方便那老师而起的名字，她另一个名字也只有上课才用。照理她父亲会用，可是他甚少有唤她的机会。大家只叫她四小姐。

老帅去年入关，赁下一座前清亲王府。偌大的地方设宴请客，盛况媲美庙会，凉棚下有杂耍的，说书的，大厅里唱京戏，内厅给女眷另唱一出，一半的院落各开着一桌麻将，后半夜还放焰火。她四处逛着，辫子上打着大的红蝴蝶结，身上的长袍是个硬邦邦的梯形，阔袖管是两个扁平而突兀的三角形，下面晃着两只手腕，看着傻相。大家说少帅同朱家姊妹亲近，常常带她们出去跳舞。他喜欢交际舞。朱三小姐是她眼中无人能及的美人儿，如果他娶的是朱三小姐那该多好！他的妻子很平凡，寡言少语，比他大四岁，相貌还要见老。幸好她极少看见他们在一起。当时还没有这样的规矩。他们有两个孩子。她父亲是四川的一个军阀，曾经救过老帅一命，老帅图报，让儿子娶了恩人的女儿。在四小姐看来这又是少帅的一个可敬之处，说起来，他是以自己的人生偿还父债。

她家里人每次提起朱家姊妹，都免不了一声嗤笑。

"野得不像样，她们的爹也不管管。一旦坏名声传出去，连小妹妹都会受连累的。'哈，就是那大名鼎鼎的朱家姊妹啊'，人家会说。"

四小姐不必提醒也会远着她们。她自觉像个乡下来的表亲。连朱五小姐都正眼看不得她。除了这一回，她问："你看见少帅没有？"

"没有。"

"找找他去。"

"什么事儿？"

"告诉他有人在找他。"

"谁呀？"

"反正不是我。"

"你自己去不行？"

"我不行。你去不要紧的。"

"你也大不了多少。"

"我看上去大。"

"我怎么知道上哪儿找去？要告诉他的又是这样没头没尾的话。"

"小鬼。人家难得托你一回，架子这么大。"朱五小姐笑着打她。

她还了手，然后跑开，"想去你自己去嘛。"

跑出了人丛，她便径直去寻找少帅。到了外面男人的世界，她要当心碰见她父亲或是异母的哥哥，贴着墙壁行走，快步躲闪到盆栽后，在回廊上游荡，装作不知道自己在哪里。在灯光下，院子里果树上的一大蓬一大蓬苍白的花影影绰绰。传菜的仆役从垂着帘幕的门洞进进出出。到处人声嗡嗡，丝竹盈耳。她是棵树，一直向着一个亮灯的窗户长高，终于够得到窥视窗内。

二

"哦，他在北京？老帅见了他了？"

"我没有听说。"

"他活动是通过老傅。"

"据说老傅跟西南那边搭上了线？"

"原来是这样。怎的，他犯得着么？"

"可不是。广州那帮人不成气候的。"

"广州已经赤化了。"

"那些俄国人越来越不像话了。"

"嘿，咱们今晚只谈风月。"

"好啊，话是你说的！你纳宠不请我们吃花酒，说说该怎么罚。"

"哈哈！打哪儿听说的？小事一桩，哪里就敢劳动诸位。"

"该罚！该罚！"

"请吃饭！让贵相好来给咱们斟酒。"

奉上了鱼翅羹。

一片"请请！请请！"声中夹杂"嗳，嗳——嗳，嗳——"的低声央告，单手挡住酒杯，不让再斟满。

酒席给外国人另备了十道菜的西餐，但是 W. F. 罗纳为防万一，自己带了一条长棍面包来。他名声够响亮，可以在这一点上放任自己特异于众。他不比同桌的中国人高大，但是身胚壮实，面容普通而和悦，头发向后直梳，高鼻梁笔直地指着前方，两条法令纹沿鼻翼两侧斜伸。他伸手拿自己的水杯。

"有外国酒。"少帅向一个仆人示意，"威士忌？香槟？"

"不用了，谢谢。我不喝酒。"

"罗纳先生从来不喝，滴酒不沾，呵呵呵！"教育部总长笑着解释。

"美国禁酒。"海军部次长说。他上过英国的海军学校。

"也禁猪肉吗？"另一个说道。

"其实来一点波特酒没关系，很温和的。"又一个说。

"你不会是禁酒主义者吧？"英国作家贵甫森－甘故作诧异。

"不是。"

"那么你一定属于你们某个神秘的教派。"

"不习惯中国菜。"另一个评道。

"也不习惯中国女人，呵呵呵！罗纳先生实在是个好人，什么样的嗜好都没有。"教育部总长说。

"不喜欢中国女人，就是不喜欢女人。"贵甫森－甘说时略一欠身。

"八大胡同代表不了中国女人。"少帅道。

"这话在理！"海军部次长说。

"可惜外国人能交往的中国女人就只有她们。"贵甫森－甘说。

"正在谈什么？"罗纳猜到话题与他有关。

"正替你的男子气概申辩。"班克罗福特说。他生于山东，父母是传教师。三个外国人席位相连，让他们有伴。

"幸好我不懂中文。"罗纳道。

"非礼勿听，非礼勿言。"少帅道。

"待了这些年，完全不懂吗？"班克罗福特道。

"一句也不懂。我不想学中文，学了反而困惑。"

"也许会抵触你本身对中国的想法。"贵甫森－甘说。这英国人略有醉意。深色眼睛长得离黑色的一字眉很近，下半张脸阔大，看上去显胖。初到中国他就赶上了拳民之乱，亲历其境，第一本书便写这题材，因此出了名。他自然受不了这美国来的新闻贩子居然也做了中国人的顾问，和他平起平坐。

"别人告诉你的许多话听不懂其实也好，"罗纳说，"有时他们只是客气，或是想博取好感。"

"他是学不了语言，只好装犬儒。"班克罗福特说。

"听说个性强的人难学会另一门语言。"少帅说。

"你呢？你觉得自己个性弱吗？"贵甫森－甘说。

"别扯上我。"

"咱们少帅的个性当然是强了。"海军部次长说，"样样都是先锋，不推牌九，打扑克牌；不叫条子，捧电影明星和交际花。"

"又来侮辱咱们的女同胞了。话说回来，咱们啥时候打扑克牌？"他用中文高声问全桌。

教育部总长一面摇头，摆摆手，"扑克牌我不敢奉陪。教育部是清水衙门。"

"是您太谦虚。"

"欸，少帅，上海有份新闻报评出了民国四公子，您是其中一位。"

他哼了一声，"民国四公子。听着真损。"

"还有哪些人？"

"有袁弘庄——"

众人略过不谈另外两个。军阀之子而已，跟他们相提并论不足恭维。

"弘庄工诗善字，但是哪比得上少帅既懂军事，又有全才。"

"如今他在上海卖条幅呢。彻底的名士派。"

"他是半个高丽人吧？他母亲是原籍高丽的两位皇贵妃之一。"

"复辟的时候你在这里么？"班克罗福特问罗纳。

"哪一次？"

"首任大总统当皇帝那一次。"

"其实整场风波是从我开始的。就是在一个这样的晚宴上，我当时说，究竟是君主制还是共和制于中国最适宜，仍然可以辩论。那些中国人全都马上说开了，从来没见过他们那样兴奋。不出几个礼拜，全国各地便纷纷成立所谓'筹安会'，鼓吹复辟了。"

他对抗了这场他引爆的运动。他帮助一个遭软禁的反对派将军藏身洗衣篮，潜逃出北京。将军鼓动其他省份起事，反对新皇帝。罗纳张罗局面让他退了位，继续做大总统。但是叛军坚持要他退休。罗纳只好抚平他对于家人与祖坟安全的忧惧，说服他辞了职。如同一个孤独的冠军，罗纳自己与自己对阵。

"对了，你家乡是在德克萨斯州吗？"贵甫森－甘问道。

他微微一笑，"不，奥克拉荷马州。"

听着传译的中国人无不殷切地定时额首，头部在空气中划出一个个圆圈。现代史没有变成史籍，一团乱麻，是个危险的题材，绝不会在他们的时代笔之于书。真实有一千种面相。

"有人说是一个妓女把他偷运出北京城的。"

海军部次长用外交辞令向罗纳补白："大家知道肯定有人帮了忙。如果是一个跟他交好的妓女，故事会更加动人。"

"所以我成了妓女了。"

"啧啧，你怎么成？"贵甫森－甘说道。

"徐昭亭在外国做什么？"罗纳问教育部总长。

"借钱呀。"

"为了通常的目的？建军。"

教育部总长呵呵笑了几声，听上去有点尴尬。徐是段执政的人。执政没有军队，但是有老帅与基督将军两座靠山，本来并不需要武备。

罗纳重新埋首于他的冷牛排。讲完某个长故事便冷不防抛出一个问题，是他的惯伎。听者一旦沉浸到安全感之中，争取注意的天性往往会浮现，答案因而更可能接近事实。

中国人似乎依然在谈论那次复辟。还有一个关于晚宴东道主和复辟的掌故，罗纳当然不会在这里讲。当时老帅已经是统兵满洲的军官，北京特意任命了一个与他相得的总督。此人是呈递秘密请愿书，呼吁恢复帝制的十四省代表之一。论功行赏，他获封一等公爵，老帅则是二等子爵，感到不满。他召集一大群军官同行去了总督的官邸，说道："大人拥立皇上有功，想必要出席登基大典。特来请大人的示，定哪一天起程，我们准备相送。"

总督自知地位不保，"我明晚进京。"

老帅奉陪到底，召集军官幕僚饯行。满洲自此再无总督。新皇帝无暇他顾。

"早在远征高丽的时候他就想做皇帝了，"海军部次长翻译道，"他在营帐里小睡，有个勤务兵进来，见到床上一只硕大无朋的蛤蟆，惊慌间打碎了一个花瓶。他没有责骂，只叫那人不要说出去。要是让满人知道他们的一个将军将来是要做皇帝的，那还了得。"

"蛤蟆是皇族的徽号吗？"贵甫森－甘问道。

"不，只要是大动物。睡梦里变成大动物据说是个征兆。实际上，肯定是那勤务兵摔碎了花瓶怕受惩罚，才编造出那样一个藉口。"

"大蛤蟆。"一屋子喃喃低语。无人敢赞赏勤务兵的急才。首任大总统的面容说穿了确实神似。

不过是会吸引外国人的那一类花哨的迷信而已，罗纳想。他对于这些据说令中国人不同的东西不耐烦，因为他知道他们没什么两样。

"这是我从他秘书处的刘子乾那儿听说的。他还真想过娶个高丽公主，将来做高丽国王。"

"因为他是河南人嘞。中原是最早的龙兴之地，那里的人满脑子帝王将相。他要是生在江南，绝不会那么大胆。"说话的是江南人氏。

"他是个十九世纪中国人，"罗纳说，"很有才干，但是早衰。五十几岁就老态龙钟，头发和胡髭全白了。他以为我是亲近国民党的，每次打招呼都说'老民党，广州有什么新闻啊？'"

"罗纳先生一肚子轶闻。"教育部总长说完又用英文复述。

"不然还有什么？"罗纳说，"二十年来只有乱纷纷的过场人物，正是轶闻里的那种脚色。"

"其实你多大年纪了？"少帅说。

"噢，我前两天看到你。"罗纳说。

"在哪儿？"

"在长城上打高尔夫球。"

他大笑，"那儿的球场非常好。"

长城内侧的绿草坡上，穿着他宽松的白色法兰绒裤子，令人一见难忘。据说他喜欢一切摩登现代的东西，在奉天学英文时一度与基督教青年会的人接近。他健谈而不甚善听，一旦感到对方在说教便一走了之。父亲矮小衰弱，杏核儿眼，胡髭下露出勉强的笑容。罗纳熟悉这种人。奥克拉荷马州当地有些大亨便出身牛仔，跟老帅一样。不，确切地说，他本是马医。满洲从前与老西部似乎很相像。马匹犁田，也用于远途骑行。他的父亲被一个赌徒杀死，为了报仇，他夜闯仇人家，误将一个女佣射死后，潜逃入伍。多年后他重返故地，很快被捕而越狱成功，给一个村庄做保险队谋生。保险队与土匪的界线并不分明，因此传说他做过胡匪，又称红胡子，也许得名于黑龙江上从事劫掠的白种人部落，但是更可能源自京剧中强盗的标准脸谱。他带着十余手下安顿下来，又派人叫来他的妻。他儿子——如今的少帅——生于一个村庄。曾经有个大帮派向他挑衅，他提议与首领决斗，那人刚一答应，老帅便拔出手枪将他击毙。就是那次的快枪替他打赢了平生第一个大仗，麾下又吸纳了百余人。

如今牛仔老了，抽鸦片，许多姨太太。他行事有他自己的一套。罗纳在这边永远不愁失业。教育部总长是前面几个政府沿用下来的旧人，老相识了，好两次要给他聘书。其实，只要是搭上了个中国官员的外国人，就能获得顾问的头衔，外加每月两百元的津贴，让他默不出声。自满清已是如此。当然像贵甫森－甘那样的顾问不会在乎那两百块钱。他新出了一本《孤独的反共者：他在远东的奋斗》，老帅付给他的润笔想必丰厚。这书由上海一家英国人的书店印行，与他别的著作不同。反共者是指老帅，他在中国独力抵挡共产主义的潮流。书中吁请西方列强不要干涉他从俄国人手里收回满洲的中东铁路。日本在东北的利益鲜有提及。是日本人委托他写的吗？总之以老帅的性格，不见得会那样相信文字的力量。罗纳脑子里打了个问号，留待日后解疑。

他看见少帅起身出了房间，顿觉一阵空虚。方才他侃侃而谈，是不是想叫少帅刮目相看？一来也是因为今晚的宴席处处使他想起复辟前夕那一次，同样的大圆桌，人语营营，蒂芙尼电灯下一片通明，房间是个红木笼子，雕花隔扇中开月洞门，低垂着杏黄丝绸的帷幔。已经是十来年前的事了，那时候他还是最年青的中国通。偶尔他也纳罕自己为什么留下来。他在这里做的无非是报导乌烟瘴气的政局，在酒席上讲讲故事，写长信给远在奥克拉荷马州库恩溪的姊妹们大谈中国政治。他在这边永远不愁生计。中国人念旧，过来人受到尊敬。眼前的权力与财势总带着几分凶险，特别是现在。但是过去，即使只是十年前，也已经醇和得令人缅怀，对首任大总统就是这样。他是军阀始祖，一手造成了现状，不单如此，作为满族人的最后一个重臣，他是合乎法统的继位者。是他促成了清朝覆灭又何妨，那是时势使然，满清无可救药也是公认的。他死后，得意门生继承事业，轮番当上大总统、总理。他们构成了唯一的合法世系。段执政是他创办的军事学校的最后一个高材士官，如今却败于出身行伍甚或草莽的新军阀手上。但是所有这些新贵都会扶持某个追随首任大总统的人，以承国脉。老帅请了段氏出山做他政府的首脑，谁都觉得，这对于老段是凄惨的降格。

"嘿，老民党！"饭桌上有人喊过来，是首任大总统对他的称呼。其余他听不懂。

"他说老民党，你的特工同事怎样了？"

"谁？"

"国姨呀。"

"国姨又是谁？"

"广州那边不是称孙文为国父吗？这样，他夫人成了国母，夫人的姐妹就是国姨啰。"

"哪一个姐妹？"

"小妹妹，在这边使美人计的那个。我们少帅看来也有意思要借联姻做国舅喽。"

"别这么大声。"有人提醒。

"走了。到北京饭店跳舞去了。"

"说来这一场南北联盟快要入港了。"另一个说道。

"她将来的嫁妆可不止两艘军舰。"

海军部次长当初带了两艘军舰从广州叛逃过来，换得官职。

"老帅的意思如何？"

"我们老帅最看重一个忠字。以他对亲家的感情，离婚绝对没戏。"

"这话最好跟那位小姐讲讲。"

有人让海军部次长给罗纳翻译。

"从她还是小女孩那时起，我就很少见到她了。"

"你是他们家的老朋友，有责任告诉他们当心小姐名节受损，叫孙博士身后蒙羞啊。"

少帅在院子里跟四小姐说话。

"谁找我？"

"不知道。"

"别跑。是谁叫你来的嘛？"

"没有谁，我高兴来就来，高兴走就走。"

"那你这么着急是要去哪儿？"

"去看戏。"

"哪一出？我跟你一块儿去。"

"人家在等你呢。"

"谁？"

"问你自己。"

"小鬼，既然你不说，我就不去了。"

"不去就不去，谁稀罕？"

"你不想让我去。"

"不识好人心。下回看看谁还肯给你带话。"

"带什么话？"

她捶他，两人在芭蕉树下扭打起来。

"回来回来，你这是去哪儿？"

"去告诉大嫂。"

谁都知道他不怕妻子。这样说吓不倒他。但是那夜迟些时候
她没见到他和朱三小姐在一起，想必他并没有来。幽会地点就是
他们俩谈话的院子，里头一屋子围在大红桌布前的猪肝色的脸，
有些人面无笑容，站着狂吼，或劝酒或推辞，或邀人划拳，这种
属于男性的仪式于她一向既怪诞，又完全无法理解，围成一圈的
红母牛被领进了某种比孔子还要古老的祭典之中。那些外国人极
力保持微笑，高高的白衣领托出灰暗的深棕色头部，像照片一样。
难怪他与外国人为伍，不和她父亲那样的人应酬往来。

她对自己的针锋相对久久不能释怀。在家里她向来很安静。
"别生事"是洪姨娘的口头禅。她生母已故，由另一侧室带大。家
里别的孩子都有人撑腰，惟独洪姨娘早已失宠。他也是幼年丧母，

由五老姨太抚养成人。

"他们家那些少爷，父亲一背转身就无法无天了。"洪姨娘说过。

"不像咱们这儿呀。"女佣也附和。

"他们是不好这些。"洪姨娘半眨了眨眼。

她们闲话从前，彼此安抚着。四小姐发现是她父亲提携了老帅。他在东北总督任上特赦了那个匪首，并任命他为统领。革命那年，总督倾向于为满人保存满洲。但是革命党在军中安插了间谍。一次军务会议上，有个军官提议效法他省宣布"同情革命"，推举总督做都督。老帅不等轮到自己便起立发言：

"我陈祖望不同情革命。"然后把枪掼在桌上。

会商无果，总督召来陈祖望，说道：

"革命党想必是决心起事了，不然也不会暴露身分。我预备随时以身殉国。"

"大人不要忧虑。我陈祖望有的正是忠心。大人的安全由我来担保。"

他调来自己的人马护卫周总督，又借他的号令部署军队。革命党人逃离了东北。然而周总督要把满洲移交肃亲王的计划被日本人挫败——可能老帅也暗中作梗。周终于放弃，在北京找了份差事。几个政府浮沉替换，他也退了休。如今人称"东北王"的老帅进兵关内。他一手造就的魔王尾随他跨入北京，虽然是一个心存感激的魔王。

四小姐听见一个异母兄说"咱们每年给肃亲王三万块钱"，诧异到极点。他们就像是那种靠丰厚的抚恤金生活的人家，旧例的开销足以维持,但抗拒任何新的支出。那一回的风波闹得沸沸扬扬,就是因为洪姨娘在院内装了一部电话,方便自己安排外出的牌局,而不必用家里公用的那部。她用的是私蓄。反对的理由是这样靡费或会招来闲话,仿佛洪姨娘也会有个相好。四小姐无法想像她从前竟是堂子中人。关于她,只知道她进堂子以前家里姓洪。四小姐记忆所及,从来就没见过她父亲踏进她们的院子。洪姨娘老得快,得以保存颜面,戴金边眼镜,穿一件黑大褂,底下棉裤的皱褶在腰间坟起。

"听说二小姐定了人家了。"一个老妈子悄声道。洪姨娘也喊喊促促回应:

"哪一家呀?"

"段家。"

"哪一房呀?"

"不知道。说是死了太太的。有肺病。"

"这些都是天注定的。男人身体好,还不是说病就病了。"

"也是啊。"

"有孩子没有?"

这些话四小姐听着愕然,但是从来没想到自己身上。她这个异母的姐姐早已成年了。盲婚如同博彩,获胜的机会尽管渺茫,究竟是每一个人都有希望,尤其在婚姻尚且遥远的时候。

她在私塾里念了首诗:

娉娉袅袅十三余,

豆蔻梢头二月初。

春风十里扬州路,

卷上珠帘总不如。

"是写给一个青楼女子的。"塾师说。

从前扬州的一个妓女,压倒群芳的美人与她竟然同龄,简直不能想像。十三岁,照现代的算法不计生年那一岁的虚龄,其实只有十二。她觉得自己隔着一千年时间的深渊,遥望着彼端另一个十三岁的人。

三

　　她磨了一个表姐过来给她做头发，单纯为了好玩，前刘海用火钳烫作卷发，堆砌成云笼雾罩的一大蓬。辫子没动，只拿粉色丝带紧紧绕了两寸长短。毛糙的巨型波浪烘托出脸庞与两根乌油油的辫子。她不知道第二天会不会去帅府，有个姨太太生日。听说老帅父子俩正在奉天，今年也许不摆酒了。她一夜伏着桌子睡觉，脸埋在肘弯里，头发微微烧焦的气味使她兴奋。

　　他在家。但是在陈家的这些热闹中常常会有这么一刻，盛大的日子在她身边荡荡流过，平滑中略有起伏，仿佛一条太阳晒暖的大河，无论做什么事都会辜负这样的时光。那些戏她全都看过了，最好的男旦压轴才上场。那丑角挥着黑扇子念出一段快板献寿，谁也不去听他。她跟着另外几个女孩子瞎逛。洛阳牡丹盆栽——据说是用牛奶浇灌的——叠成的一座假山，披挂着一串串五彩电灯泡，中间摆得下一张饭桌。今天变魔术的是个日本女人，才在上海表演过的，想必精彩。她们在少帅书房里议论戏码单，他好奇地瞥了她两眼，然后几乎再不看她。是头发的缘故。她顶着那个热腾腾的云海，沁出汗珠来。几个月不见，她现在大了，他不再逗她了。朱家姊妹不在，其他女孩子也都没什么话说。他把别人从杭州捎给他的小玩意分赠她们。

"咱们走吧，魔术师该上场了。"一个女孩子说。

她正要跟着出去，他说："这柄扇子是给你的。"

她展开那把檀香扇，端详着。

"现在是大姑娘了，不再搭理人了。"

"啊？"

"而且这么时髦。要定亲了。"

"哪儿来的这些昏话？"她不禁红了脸。他以前从来不和她开这种玩笑，老太太们才喜欢这样说。

"你不肯说。喜酒也不请我吃啰？"

"别胡说。"听上去不像是戏言了。临头灾祸陡然举起她，放到成年人中间。

"唔？那我等着吃喜酒了。"

"呸！"她作势一啐，转身要走，"你今天怎么了？"

"好好，对不起，是我多管闲事。"

"这些话都是打哪儿来的？"

"你真没听说？"她第一次看见他眼睛里有焦急的神色，一闪而过。

"没有的事儿。"

"唐家人正在给你说媒。"

"没这事儿。反正我不会答应的。"

他笑了，"你不答应有什么用？"

"杀了我也不答应。"机会来了，为他而死并表明心迹。

"不如告诉他们说五老姨太认了你做女儿，你的终身有她来安排。"

"我永远不结婚。"

"为什么？"

"不想。"

"那你一辈子做老姑娘是要干什么呢？上大学？出洋？做我的秘书陪我一道出洋，好不好？你在看什么？"他凑近看看折扇上究竟有什么东西让她着迷。

"我在数数儿。"

"数什么？"

"美人儿。"

他逐一点算花园中亭子里的彩绘人物，"十。"

"十一。"

"应该是十二。通常有十二个。"

"窗子里的这个我数漏了。正好是十二。"

"这个我数过。这儿，树后面还有一个。"

"一、二、三、四……"她数出十个。

靠得这样近，两人都有些恍惚，每次得到的数目都不同。他终于一把捉住她，轻轻窘笑了一声，"这儿还有另一个。"

"让我数完。"

"这儿的一个呢？一丁点儿大，刚才都没看见。"

他不放开她的手腕，牵起来细看，"怎么这么瘦？你从前不是这样的。"

她立即羞愧自己始终没长到别人期望的那么美，只好咕哝一句："只不过是最近。"

"最近不舒服吗？"

"不，只是没胃口。"

"为什么？"

她不答。

"为什么？"

她越是低着头，越是觉得沉重得无法抬起头来。

"不是因为我吧？"

他撩起她的前刘海，看她脸上被掩映的部分。她一动不动，迎风光裸着。他的手臂虚虚地笼着她，仿佛一层粉膜。她惘然抵抗着。他一定也知道是徒然。由于他们年岁的差别，他很早以前就娶了亲，犹如两人生在不同朝代。她可以自由爱恋他，仿佛他是书里的人。不然她怎会这样不害臊？她忽然苦恼：如果他不懂，她不知道如何才说得明白。他又怎能猜到？跑开只会显得是假装羞涩。她跑了，听见那扇子在脚下嘎吱一响。

出了那房间，她很快便放慢脚步，免得被人瞧见。他没有追随她。她既如释重负又异常快乐。他爱她。随他们说媒去，发生什么她都无所谓了。他爱她，永远不会改变。居然还是下午，真叫人惊异。舞台上的锣声隐隐传来。她寂寞得很，只能去触摸游廊上的每一根柱子每一道栏杆。又拐了个弯,确信他不会看见之后，她的步子跳跃起来，只为了感受两根辫子熟悉的拍打落在肩膀上，不知为何，却像那鸣锣一样渺茫了。

四

"帅府五老姨太派了部汽车来接四小姐。"她父亲的院子差人来传话。

一个男仆领着她去少帅的书房。她停在门口微笑。

"进来，进来。你来了真好。今儿有空，带你看看网球场，刚盖好的。会打网球吗？"

"不会。"

"乒乓球一定会的。"

"不会。"

那男人还会端茶回来。他们默默坐着等待，他低着头，脸上一丝微笑，像捧着一杯水，小心不泼出来。

那人终于送来了茶，退了出去。

"我有个消息跟你说。"

"上回准是你的把戏。"

"过来这边坐，你不想人家听见的。"

"谁要听这些昏话？"

"啧，人家替你担心哪。你听见什么没有？"她摇了摇头。"那就好。"

"全是你编出来的。"

"不要没良心。你知道为什么从此不提了？我叫人向那边透了点口风，所以他们才会作罢。"

"你跟他们说什么了？"

"说你已经许给另一家了，不然呢？"

她拿拳头捶他，"老实说，你是怎么讲的？"

"不过是说五老姨太已经替你想好了一门亲事，只是你还太小，还得等几年。"

"爹要是听说了怎么办？"

"有什么关系？那也并不过分。"

"也许他们就不许我上这儿来了。"

"如果你不来，我带枪上你家去。"

她希望自己被囚禁，那么他就会为了她而来，"你不过是说笑。"

"不。"

他把她拉到膝上。她低头坐着，感到他的双眼在自己的脸旁边发亮，像个耳坠子一样。他顺着气息将她吸进去。即使他们只能有这样的刹那又如何，她想，已经仿佛一整天了。时间缓慢下来，成了永恒。

"你的眉是这样走的。"她一只手指追踪着，拂过随触随合的眼皮，再小心翼翼沿鼻梁而下，检点每一件东西，看自己买了什么。他看起来焕然一新。一拥有就不同了，正如画片有别于书里的插图。

"你没去过北戴河？青岛还要好。咱们要去那里。你学游泳。能这样抱着你睡一晚就好。"

她的微笑僵了一点。

"光是抱着。我小时候有一回出去打猎，捉到一只鹿，想带回家养，抱着它在地上滚来滚去，就是不松手。最后我困得睡着了，醒过来它已经跑了。"

她紧搂着他，要挤掉他胳臂间的空虚。

"它挺大的，比我那时候大多了。"

"你那时候有枪吗？"

"没有，还不让我带枪。只有弓箭和一把小刀。"

"那是在东北。"

"嗯，是很好的猎场。"

"天气非常冷吗？"她父亲做东北总督时，母亲就在当地的堂子里。她自幼只有父亲，从未觉得自己是半个东北人。其实她长得相当像他，同样是长而直的眼睛，鹅蛋脸五官分明。他退开一点，微笑看着她。

"真想吃了你，可是吃了就没有了。"

"有人来了。"她听见院子里有声。

"这儿没有人来。"

"那天我们大家都在这里。"

"我单独在这儿的时候不会放人进来的。"

单独与某人相对？比如朱三小姐吗？已经不重要了。在一个乱糟糟的世界，他们是仅有的两个人，她要小心不踩到散落一地的棋子与小摆设。她感觉自己突然间长得很高，笨拙狼狈。

"少帅，上头有请。"一个声音从走廊尽头喊来。

他父亲要他应酬访客。他去了差不多一个钟点才回来，又把她放在膝头，抚摸她的脚踝。傍晚他再一次给叫了去。不一会仆人过来说，汽车会载她回家。

下趟五老姨太请她过去，汽车驶进一条僻静的街，拐进长胡同，停在一幢她从未见过的宅子前面。汽车夫打开车门。她略一踌躇，便用头巾掩面，像乘坐黄包车的女人要挡住尘沙。她带着这张轻纱般的鸭绿色的脸走进去，经过一群穿制服的卫兵，他们在前院外一间亮着灯的房里打麻将。他在下一进院子里等着她。

"这是谁的房子？"

"我的。总得有个去处才行，家里没一刻清静。"

"我不知道你有自己的房子。"

"没机会常来，所以是这个样子。带你走走吧。"

"这里没有别人？"

"没有。"

好像在一幢荒废的房子里扮家家酒。每个半空的房间要怎样处置，他们俩都很有想法。卧室倒是家具齐全。窗帘低垂，梳妆台上的瓶瓶罐罐在半黑中闪烁着。

"谁住这里？"

他很快地关了门，"这间是客房，有时我会叫一帮朋友过来通宵打扑克牌。旁边这个房间有一张炕，我打算拆了铺上地板，以后咱们就可以跳舞了。"

他们走了一圈。

"朱三小姐常来？"

"唔，来过一两回。"

之后她不大说话。回到客厅，他说："你不一样。我们会永远在一起的。"

"不能。"

"为什么？"

"你太太。"

"那只是为了老帅。我一向没亏待她，毕竟当初也不是她的主意。我同她会达成某种安排的，不过由我和老帅谈就行了。"他向来称"老帅"，仿佛他只是他父亲的一个部将。孝顺是旧派的美德，使他有点难为情，他喜欢归之于军纪。

"现在马上说什么是没用的，你年纪太小。只会害你被囚禁。"

"你说过你会带枪来救我。"

"对老丈人最好还是不要用枪。"

她笑着扭身脱开。不知为什么，这新的前景并没有使她惊异。他们的无望于她本来就不是什么藉口，如今更抛诸脑后。他也爱她；有了这个神奇的巧合，什么事都有可能。

"我不想要这里，可是很难找到另一处既近帅府，又不喧闹。还要有地方安置卫队。"

"他们要是去帅府接我怎么办？"

"会给我打电话的。到时再过去也不晚。"

"痒。"她捺住顺着她的漏斗形袖管摸索的手。

"你怎么穿了这许多衣服？今天太晚了，改天我开汽车带你去西山。"

"你会开汽车？"

"很容易的。"

"我们可以在西山骑毛驴儿。"

"我们租来骑。我挺想在西山住的。那外国新闻记者罗纳在西山有幢别墅，盖在过去禁苑里的一座佛寺上头。最近他才说起来。第一次直奉战争的时候，他在西山前线四处走动，看见地上有一根弯弯曲曲的电线，捡了起来，边走边绕线团。我们有几个人走过去冲他呼喝。他只是竖起大拇指说：'老帅很好。'然后摇头：'吴蟠湖不好。'他们笑着放他走。这一来战地电话被切断，东北军后撤，局势翻转了。所以照他说，是他害我们打了败仗。"

"他不怕讲出来？"

"他邀我作客，看他电铃上缠着我们的电线。这些洋人自以为多么勇敢。他们一走进枪林弹雨马上就停火了，怕杀掉一个洋人。除了在中国，哪里有这种绝对安全的历险呢？"

"他们说你喜欢洋人。"

"跟他们一起很高兴。比较坦率。我最讨厌拍马屁的。"他探身掸了掸烟灰，别过头来吻她，一只鹿在潭边漫不经心啜了口水。额前垂着一绺子头发，头向她俯过来，像乌云蔽天，又像山间直罩下来的夜色。她晕眩地坠入黑暗中。

仍旧是有太阳的下午天，四面围着些空院子，一片死寂。她正因为不惯有这种不受干涉的自由，反觉得家里人在监视。不是她俨然不可犯的父亲，在这种环境根本不能想像；是其他人，总在伺机说人坏话的家中女眷，还有负责照顾她的洪姨娘与老妈子。她们化作朴拙的、未上漆的木雕鸟，在椽子与门框上歇着。她没有抬头，但是也大约知道是圆目勾喙的雌雄，一尺来高，有的大些，有的小些。她自己也在上面，透过双圈的木眼睛俯视。他的手拉扯着她的裤管与丝绸长衬裤，心不在焉地褪下长统袜。坐在他身上使她感到极其怪异，仿佛有一个蒙着布的活塞，或是一条挥打着的返祖般的尾巴，在轻轻捶击她。小时候老妈子们给她讲过脊柱下端尾骨的笑话，也让她摸过自己的尾骨。"这是割掉尾巴以后剩下来的。人从前有尾巴。"尽管暗地里仿佛还没有完，她依然疑心不是真的。她不想问他，大概总与性有关。也许只有置之不理才不失闺秀风度。

从黄昏开始，鼓楼每隔半个钟点擂八下鼓。钟楼随即响应，宣告夜晚与道德宵禁的来临。

"我以前居然没注意到，"她说，"听上去像古时候。"

"钟鼓楼是明朝建的。"

"从那时候起每天晚上都这样吗？"

"嗯，满人也照旧。"

"我们为什么还要这样？现在有时钟了。"

"可不是吗？民国建立十五年了，还是什么都没变。"

他拉铃绳，脚步声近了便喊"摆饭"。在隔壁房间晚膳，左右无人。他捧着饭碗向她微笑。只他两人同台吃饭，终于真的当家了。她窘得百般纠结，只得放下饭碗。

"怎么了？"

"没什么。你吃。"

一块洒了古龙水的新毛巾架在边桌的热水盆上保温。他吃完饭，她便浸了浸毛巾，绞干给他，才递过一半已经转身要走，觉得自己在服侍丈夫似的，不由得难为情。她侧身避开回头微笑，倏然串成一个动作。他着迷地捉住她的手，但她抽回去了。

"出来吧。"他唤道。

他们在游廊上望月。他搂着她，腰间暖意像风中火焰一样拂拭她的背脊，使她诧笑。大红柱子映出蓝色的月光。

"想想真是，我差点儿回不来了。"

她抓紧他，"什么时候？上回你在奉天时？"

"唔，出了事，我们有个军官倒戈，基督将军也在里头。"

"我好像听说关外打仗了。"

"是差点儿打起来了。我们的主力部队开赴奉天，离城只有几里。老帅的专列上东西堆得满坑满谷，预备随时开走。"

"去哪儿？"

"大连。"

"大连……那是你本来要去的地方。"

"是要去。那时候我跟奉天断了联系。甚至有谣言说我也是叛党。"

"怎么会这样？"她小声说。

"就因为姓顾的和我看法相近，关系也不错。"

"他们怎么能说这种话？你自己的父亲。老帅不信吧？"

"老帅非常生气。"

"可是……现在好了？"

"现在不提了。当然我也有错，应该更留神的。"

因此他更有理由不对他父亲提出她的事或是任何要求，至少在目前。但是这又算得了什么，根本比不上他们俩几乎失之交臂的恐怖，想想已经觉得心寒，仿佛他整个人就在她眼前瓦解，在指缝间溜走。但是这张蓝光勾画的脸就在这里，向她俯视微笑，嘴唇冷冰冰压上来。他就在北京城这里，钟鼓延续着夜更，外头声音更大，黑夜的奇异与危机更觉迫切。古城后千回百转的时光兔窟和宫殿都在刹那间打通，重门一道一道訇然中开，连成一个洞穴或隧道。

"你该走了，"他说，"我们不要坐一辆汽车。"

"五老姨太这样喜欢你，怎不认你做女儿？"洪姨娘说。

"我不想。"

"傻孩子。有个富有的干妈多好。她会给你找到一户好人家的。"

"洪姨娘从来没一句正经话。"她向前一倒，下颔抵在桌子上，玩弄手边的小物件。

"倒真是。指望你爹呗，就拿你做人情送出去了。当然这是我跟你讲体己话。"

"你尽管扯，谁要听。"

"我知道你不会说的。"

是话里有话？不会的，她很快把这想法排斥到意识外。

"你洪姨娘没说什么？"他问。

"没。"

"要是他们知道你到这儿来，孤男寡女，一定会认为你给占便宜了。有吗？"他笑着把脸凑上去看她，她一再躲避，"有吗？"

她蜷曲身子紧挨沙发边。

"要是他们真问你了你怎么说？"

"照实说。"

"那么再把你嫁出去也还不晚。"

"那我就说谎。"她隔了一会儿说。

"没有用的。呵，真是没办法了我就把你劫走。"

"老帅会气得不得了。"

"一定的。他特别敬重你父亲。"

"咱们该怎么办？"

"没关系，反正我跟老帅已经很僵了。"

她不喜欢与他并躺在沙发上，但是这样可以久久凝视彼此的脸。只恨每人多生了一条胳臂。几次三番藏掖不了，他说："砍掉它。"下午的阳光往墙上的镜子投下一道小彩虹。她仿佛一辈子也没有感受过这样的平静安稳。沙发靠背是地平线上遥遥起伏的山峦，在金色沙漠般的沉静中，思想纹丝不动。房间里开始暗下来了。她的微笑随暮色转深，可怕的景象令他眯萋着眼。他把脸埋进她披拂的、因结辫而卷曲的头发里。

"不知为什么，你刚才像一个鬼。"

"哪一种鬼？"

"寻常的那种。有男人迷了路，来到荒郊野外的一幢大宅前，给请进去跟漂亮的女主人吃晚饭。共度一宵后，他走出宅外回头一看，房子没有了，原先的地方只有一座坟山。"

可见他跟她一样害怕这道门内的一切都是假的。

"有一种无日无夜的感觉，只有一个昏暗的黄褐色太阳，好像在阴间。"

"那是因为我们成天关在这儿。"

"我一辈子没有跟谁这么长时间待着。"他窘笑，"人家问我这些天都忙什么去了，怎么总不见影儿。"

"不知道他们在你背后怎么说。"

"我恨不得告诉他们。"

"要是他们说我是你的丫头，我也不管。"

丫头比姨太太容易说出口。但即使她一面说一面连自己也感动，意识深处还是有一丝怀疑。也许她随时能够叫一声"骗你的！"然后笑着冲出去。她随时可以停止。她会坐到他怀里，纽扣解开的袄子前襟掩人耳目地留在原位，松开的裤头与没有打结的裤带一层层堆在腰际。他沿着暖热的皱褶一路摸索下去，她躲在壁橱里等待被发现，有一阵莫名的恐惧。每一下抚摸就像悸动的心跳，血液轰隆隆地流遍她，浑身有一阵倾听的静默。彼此的脸咫尺天涯，都双目低垂，是一座小庙的两尊神像，巍巍然凸出半身在外，正凝望一个在黑暗中窥探肚脐上红宝石洞眼的窃贼。

他的头毛茸茸的摩擦着她裸露的乳房，使她有点害怕和恶心。她哪里来的这样一个吮奶的成年儿子？她见他首先空洞地瞥一眼起了鸡皮疙瘩的粉色乳头，然后才含进嘴里。那痒丝丝的吸吮又在不断磨擦她，针刺她，仿佛隔着一层金属筛网在挤压。他转向另一边时，她低头看看那个缓缓平伏的苍白小三角形，不无忧虑。他终于惘然地抬头，眼睛红光迷离，重新拣起香烟。她拉直衣服，走到镜子前整理刘海。在那片回复原状的黑色大方块的遮蔽下，她对他微笑，又向下伸展手臂，十指相扣像忍住一个呵欠似的，以掩饰轻微的狼狈。这动作使她的衣袖像亭子的檐角一样挑起来，裤管下也露出白色 L 形的脚，绣鞋、袜子全是白的。他伸一伸手，也没抬高，她立即又回到他旁边。

两性间的基本法则她一窍不通，连赤条条躺在他的身躯下，也觉得随时可以起来走开。在她的重负中间有一只袋，软笃笃轻柔柔，形成一个令她不安的真空。她的手来回摸索他窄窄的背脊，但是他一冲动起来她便沉着脸，僵着身体。应当等到"洞房花烛"——追溯到穴居时代的新婚夜。如果她不为那晚保留什么，连他也会责怪她。而且如果哪天——虽然她尽量不让自己这样想——她一踏出这道门，这房子就变作坟山呢？这里发生的只存在于他们两人之间，一旦回到外面各自生活，便会消融得无影无踪了。

他想起有一个推不掉的约会。汽车会回来接她。她后来意识到他有点生气，感到忽忽若失。

"只有这办法。过后谁也奈何不了我们了。"他说。

她一张脸别开枕在沙发靠垫上，微微点头。他们一直没有走近卧室。

"嗳，办不到的。"她带笑说道，仿佛是要她吞下一只瓶，甚至于一个有圈形凸纹的陶罐。

"疼。"

"马上就不疼了。"他停下好几次。

"不行，还是疼。"

"我们今天要办完它。"

还在机械地锤着打着，像先前一样难受，现在是把她绑在刑具上要硬扯成两半。突然一口气冲上她的胸口。就在她左一下右一下地晃着头时，只见他对她的脸看得出神。

"我觉得要吐出来了。"

他又再不停吻她，赶紧回到正事，古来所谓的鱼水之欢和鸳鸯交颈舞。不如说是一条狗在自顾自地撞向树桩。她忍不住大笑，终于连泪水也笑出来了。他苦笑，泄了气。他又再撑起四肢蹲伏，最后一轮细察了地面，才伸直身子来轻吻她，搂她入怀。

"也算是做完了。"他仿佛借此下台似的说。

回复平静后，他们难得又可以假装能一觉睡到天明。她诧异他睡着了。落地灯黄黯的光线下，这个陈设西洋家具的中式房间起了奇异的变化。熟悉的几案橱柜全都矮了远了，贴墙而立，不加入战斗。他蜷身侧卧，忽然看上去很平凡，很陌生，是新造的第一个男子，可以是任何人，根本不值得费那么多工夫来制作。

然而每一次重见都如隔数年，她又一而再地变了。他们向对方咧嘴一笑，心照不宣。因此也不会一块儿坐，也尽说些闲话。他拉她站起来的时候，她说不要，会疼的。

"我们一定要搞好它。"

他拉着她的手往沙发走去。仿佛是长程，两人的胳臂拉成一直线，让她落后了几步。她发现自己走在一列裹着头的女性队伍里。他妻子以及别的人？但是她们对于她没有身分。她加入那行列里，好像她们就是人类。

五

"这两天风声不好。"洪姨娘与老妈子们窃窃议论。

她以为东北打完仗了？传说北京城外发生了刺杀。谁也不出门，正门上了闩，还用大水缸顶住。如果少帅的汽车来过接她，也没有人跟她说。

她已经就寝了，照顾她的老妈子走进来，神色郑重地悄声说："少帅来了。"

他在门外。她连忙穿衣服。

"吃惊吧？"

她只说了声"这么晚！"仿佛除此以外在卧室会见男客也没什么不妥。老妈子走了，得体地虚掩房门。

"你怎么进来的？"

"闯进来的。告诉过你如果你不来，我会闯来嘛。"

"瞎说。"

但是他一身军服，手枪插在枪套里。

"前院知道吗？"

"我从离你最近的那个后门进来的，他们不会知道。一个仆人开的门，他认得我是谁。"

见到他仗着权势施展穿墙过壁的魔法，她禁不住兴奋。在这个房间见到他，有一种异样的感觉——这里于她早已经太小了，近乎破落，只有童年的颓垣败瓦散满一地。但是她庆幸可以打破咒语，不再受困于他们的鬼屋。他们出来了，这里是日常世界。在这房间里她曾经对他百般思念，难道他看不出？常有时候她夜里从帅府的寿宴回来，难得看到他一眼，然而感受却那么深刻，那么跟她的旧房间格格不入，以至她只能怔怔望着窗子，仿佛在听音乐。微弱的灯光映在黑漆涂金木框内空空的黑色窗格上，泛棕褐色。她不走到窗边，只正对窗前站着，任一阵湿风像围巾般拂拭她的脸，这时候现实的空气吹着面颊，浓烈的感觉弥漫全身，随又松开，无数薄器皿的图案散去，欢乐的歌声逐渐消散。相比那样喧腾的感觉之河，他来到这里的真身只像是鬼魂罢了。

"是不是要打仗了？"

"现在传言很多。"

那老妈子会不会端茶过来，把会客的幌子维持下去？难说。也许这会儿正在生炉子。

"大家都锁起门来待在家里？"

"怕遇上抢劫。"

"他们是怕谁？基督将军已经跑了。"

"冯还有部队在这里。在西城门。"

势力较弱的基督将军怎么会是老帅的长期盟友，她一直不大明白，他们决裂后的情形更加使她困惑。

"被刺杀的是谁？"

"徐昭亭。"他望着别处咕哝道。又是一个不需要她记住的人名。"冯干的。"

"在火车上。"

"嗯，我差点坐了同一趟车。"他带笑说。

"啊？"他的另一个世界，那个由无数难记的人名和沉闷的政治饭局汇聚而成的大海，突然波涛汹涌地掩没了房间。

"给徐昭亭送行的饭局我也在座，他叫我跟他一块儿坐火车，反正我本来也要去趟天津的。他们原定在铁轨上埋伏炸药，不过运兵车太多，没法下手。最后他们把他拽下了火车。这一来都知道是谁干的了。"

"你没去真是万幸。"

"所以我想，不管了，既然想见你我就要过来。"

她报以微微一笑。那老妈子还回不回来？

"老帅生气吗？"

"当然气。首都附近出了这种事。"

"会不会打起来？"

"现在人心惶惶。段执政辞职了。徐是他的人，刚从国外考察回来。"

他起身关上房门。

"别，你还是走吧。"

"现在走，和之后走一样坏。"

她看着他把皮带挂到床阑干上，那球根状铁枝残留着一圈圈褪了色的金漆，映衬出手枪的皮套，恍若梦境。

"洪姨娘肯定会听到的。"

"她大约已经知道了。"

"她不知道。"

"大家都睡下了。"

"她能看见我这边还亮着灯。"

"关掉。"

"别关。我想看见你，不然不知道是什么人。"

他面露不悦。除了他还可能有其他人？但是她要看见他的脸，像一朵从大海冒出的莲花般降临，不然就无法知道发生什么事，只会在黑暗中觉得痛。蚊帐半掖着，以便在紧急关头他可以抓起手枪。要是让人知道了洪姨娘会怎样？老妈子呢？她在害人，叫她们以后没法在这家里有口饭吃。这是罪过，却又奇异地安全，仿佛钻进阁楼里藏身。难得这次他们有一整夜的时间，就像对于院落的鸣虫来说，这已经是一生一世。她喜欢那第一下接触，仿佛终于拥有着他，一根软而滑的肉饵在无牙的噬嗑间滑出，凉飕飕的，挑逗得她膝盖一阵酥麻。但是立即转为疼痛。

"给我说个好听的就可以马上完了。说你是陈叔覃的人。"

不知怎么她就是说不出口。

"说你喜欢我。"

"我喜欢你。我喜欢你。"

他立即发了疯似的快马加鞭，背部中了一箭，哼哧哼哧喘着气还是驰骋不休，末了俯身向前，仍旧不松开，一股热的洪流从他体内涌出。

"有蚊子。"

"咬到了？在哪儿？"他用指尖蘸了唾沫，揉搓那块地方。

她微笑。一定是他小时候在乡下学的。他们还是安全地身在半夜。他是一件她可以带上床的玩具，枕边把玩的一块玉。关了灯，她只依稀能辨认他仰卧的侧影。

"你没有我那么快乐。"她觉得他面带愁容。

"因为我年纪比较大。像个孩子哭了半天要苹果，苹果拿到手里还在抽噎。"

"你一直要什么有什么。"

"不是的。"

可惜她不能走进他没有她的那些年：一个个荒凉的庭院，被古老的太阳晒成了黄色。她要一路跑进去，大声喊着"我在这儿！我在这儿呀！"

他从床边探下身去，在蚊香盘上点燃香烟。

"今晚饭桌上谈的都是徐昭亭。"

"究竟为什么要杀他？"

"他在拉拢各路人马结盟对付基督将军。他回来的时候东南那边接驾似的欢迎他。不过哪里都很把他当一回事儿。他在英国应邀出席阅兵典礼，观礼台上只有给英皇和皇后坐的两把椅子，他看了脸色很不高兴。于是乔治五世起身让他和玛丽皇后并坐，自己跟军官们站在一起。"

"他是军人吗？"

"外国人叫他徐将军。他们把谁都称作将军。其实他是个政客。小胖子。白金汉宫有一次开园游会，他的高级秘书带太太出席，那女人年过五十了，裹小脚，穿中国衣裳，但是她丈夫要她戴一顶很大的簪花草帽。有个年青的秘书不赞成，可是那高级秘书是前清的举人，天下事无所不晓，说'哪有外国妇女白天出门不戴帽子的？'离御帐大约有六百码的路，那女人小脚走不快，风还把她的帽子吹跑了。那年青秘书追赶帽子，可帽子在风里忽左忽右，忽上忽下，好一会儿才抓住。乔治五世捧着肚子哈哈大笑。"

她竭力压低笑声不让外面听见。他拉过她的手，覆住那沉睡的鸟，它出奇地驯服和细小，带着皱纹，还有点湿。

"过后徐昭亭跟那年青人说：'你大概没有考虑吧，这对英皇是大不敬。'那秘书说：'那么那美国首席大法官呢？他拍着英皇的背，一边跺脚一边大笑。'徐没再说什么。第二天伦敦《泰晤士报》讲了追帽子的新闻，没加评论，但是批评了休斯大法官，尽管他是英皇的老朋友。"

"他们还去了哪些地方？"

"美国。哪里都去到了。徐在苏联跟他们外长齐翟林舌战了一场。那边是以接待国家元首的礼数欢迎他。"

"为什么？"

"中国人除非是军人，否则谁也不把你当真。徐是北洋耆老。"

"我想去看看巴黎和意大利。"

"咱们会去的。过两年吧。"

又在播鼓撞钟了，每半个钟点一次的报时。钟鼓楼依然在中国深处，警报着黑夜的危险，直通千百年前，一分钟比一分钟深入和古老。

"老段拍电报到上海叫他不要回来。老段替他担心。但是他想，堂堂专使不敢回京覆命，势成国际笑话。再说东北在打仗，他也想趁机捞一把，那老狐狸。他觉得这是老段的机会。于是他向天津英国领事馆借了一辆汽车，车头扬着英国国旗开到北京。这次不知怎么他没有提防。命中注定的。"

"坐上火车就去了。"

"嗯，叫是叫专列，不过是普通火车上拖一节车厢。每停一站都有军乐队欢迎他，还要等很长时间给引擎加水。车站灯火通明，被兵士层层围住，就像莫斯科欢迎他的仪式那么隆重。有个军官上了火车，说要找徐先生。他秘书说专使身体不舒服，让来客坐上座，但是他坐了下首。"

"火车也分上座下座？"

"也不是卧铺。我们中国人嘛，总是先礼后兵。所以他们便聊了起来，军官说他是张督办派来的，问徐先生在哪里。秘书咬定他身体不适。徐喝多了，在另一节车厢睡觉，被说话声吵醒了，揉着眼睛走了出来。秘书说：'怎么样，我说专使身体不舒服吧？'"

他把她的手拉回来。

"那军官站了起来。徐终于让他们都重新坐下，然后说：'我身体抱恙，一路上只好谢绝招待。'张督办已经等了一晚上，还请徐先生赏光。''没有工夫。''火车多停一会儿无妨。''我得了重感冒，改天再拜访督办吧。''司令部特为准备了茶话会欢迎徐先生。''半夜三更开什么茶话会？''有急事洽商。''什么事那么急？我已经派人到蒙古和冯先生洽商一切了。'那秘书插话说：'冯先生徐先生都是一家人，无事不好商量。'但是那军官扬一扬手巾示意，立即有十几个兵士拥上车厢，扶着徐下了火车。"

"怎么他们在附近还有司令部？"

"他们是沿着铁路来摆平各样事情的。"

她永远没法明白两个军阀怎么可以各据一条铁路分治北京，而且刚打完一仗，一方竟会容许另一方这样悠然撤退。

"他们在司令部枪毙了他？"

"不不，在田地里，趁黑干的。已经够骇人听闻的了。基督将军气得直跺脚，他们把他的计划搞砸了。"

这些人变了小小的殉葬俑，青绿釉的袄子底下穿着黄裤子，打着敝旧的陶土补丁，他们俩可以把头靠在同一张枕席上仔细观看。

"老段自己惹的祸。他向来利用老冯对我们玩弄手腕，事变吓得他胆战心惊，看见老冯坐困蒙古，几十万部队军心离散，不知道他下一步要怎样。结果老冯做了这件事。他听说老段几天没去办公，可把他逼急了，便干掉了老头子最得力的副手。老段失了臂膀，怕他怕得要死，连自己家里都不敢大声说话。"

"他在蒙古也会听到？"

"他到处安插了特务，对谁都跟踪。我今晚在这里他也会知道。"

她触了一下电，想到基督将军是替他们保密的心腹好友，几乎暖在心头。

"你出去的时候没有危险吗？"

"没有。"

"不会打仗吧？"

"估计还要有一场决战。"

"因为刺杀的事？"

"反正是徐一死，他搞的反共同盟看起来就要实现了。大家都想倒冯。"

"他又信基督教，又是共产党。"

"他是伪装的。苏联每个月给他六万，还不计他拿到的军械。"

"那么他并不真的是共产党，只是假扮出来的？"

"也不见得好多少。大家说起赤祸，都说是洪水猛兽。照我看来一个大家挨穷的国家里有别的东西更可怕。大概对于年纪大的人来说，共产就是什么准则都不要了。比方说老帅，他就恨共产党。"

"这些人不很多？"

"我们抓到的就不少。也有些是大学生，真可惜他们被苏联利用了。"

"他们被抓到就只有死了。"

"嗯。"

她见过犯人的首级，偶尔吊挂在城门旁电线杆上。"不要看。"坐黄包车或是汽车路过的时候老妈子会这样说。她只有一个印象，仿佛是发根把五官全都拉扯得翘了起来，如同箍着网巾的京剧脚色，腮颊与额头上一道道红痕也像是舞台化妆。她害怕，好在没人知道是谁……洗衣的老妈子李婆有一回讲起她村里有人被捕。当夜大家都在院子里乘凉，老妈子们坐小板凳，四小姐躺在竹榻上，平滑的床板如墓碑般冰冷。黑沉沉一大片的星空朝她压下来，是一个正在塌陷的穹顶，硕大无朋，看得她眼花缭乱。她很想找到古诗所谓的"北斗阑干"。那个夏夜尽管就在外头的同一个院子里，可是已经好像过了一千年。

"他们抓他的时候他正在卖糖人儿，直接逮到司令部去了。到处抓人呐。"

"如今就是这样。"另一个老妈子感叹。谈起时事，每个人都哑着嗓子小声说话。

"听他们讲这事儿都吓死了。问斩那天，判官坐在公案后面，前边站两行扛着来福枪的兵。那四个人犯跪成一排。斩条贴在竹签上，放在公案上。判官查对了姓名，拿起毛笔在一张斩条的名字上勒一道朱红，像投枪似的投到地上，这时候兵士们就大吼一声。有个兵捡了斩条插到人犯的衣领后面，四个人都这样对上了号。突然间判官踢翻了桌子，一转身跑了。要把煞吓走。"

"煞是什么？"四小姐说。其他人都讪讪地笑。

"没听说过归煞？"洪姨娘道，"人死了，三天之后回来。"

"煞是鬼？"

"或许是地府的凶神吧。我也不大清楚。问李婆。"

"他们说呀是一只大鸟。归煞那天大家躲起来避邪。但是有些好事的人在地上撒了灰，过后就有鸟的爪子印。"

"据说呀但凡有杀人，甚至只是有杀人的念头，煞都会在附近。"洪姨娘道，"所以那个判官要保护他自己。"

她已经坐直了身子，庆幸自己在黑暗中被熟人包围着。

"人犯上身剥光了在骡车上游街，前边一队兵，后边一队兵，两边又各有两行兵。监斩官骑马跟在最后，肩膀上一条大红绸子挂下来，新郎倌儿一样。两个吹喇叭的开道，吹的是外国兵冲锋的调子，'哒哒啲哒哒啲'。兵士们齐声喊'杀啊！'看热闹的也跟着喊'杀啊！'"

"啧！这些人。"一个老妈子说。

另一个短促地笑了一声，"门房里老是有人说'看砍头去'。"

"这些男人呵！而且成天没事闲着，哪像我们。"

"讲下去呀，李婆。后来呢？"四小姐说。这话她们听了也笑。

"后来？后来那四个人在城门外跪成一排。刽子手走到第一个跟前，先用力拍了拍他脖子后面估摸尺寸，大刀一落，头踢到一边。轮到第四个，就是那和我同村的，他看了前面那些，昏过去了。醒来就躺在牢房地上。他是陪斩的。"

"陪斩的？"洪姨娘疑惑地咀嚼这几个字，"唔，有人做贵宾，有人只是请来陪他的。"

"过了几天就把他放了。到底也不大肯定他是奸细。"

"那怎么不继续关在牢里？"四小姐说。

"让他长年累月白吃白喝呀？他们就是想吓唬吓唬他。不过他回了家没几个月就死了。"

"吓破了胆，难怪的。"洪姨娘道。

"嘻呀，现在这时世还是深宅大院里好，"李婆道，"听不见外边的事儿。"

虽然这故事早于他的时代，她不知怎么并不愿意告诉他。那一定是吴蟠湖的时候。现在做法肯定不一样了吧？可是一说起其实什么都不会改变，他就难免恼火。

他把烟灰弹到地板上的蚊香盘里。"小声说了半天，喉咙都说疼了。"

"我们别说话了。"

"那样会睡着的。"

"也许你最好现在走，趁着天没亮。"

他忖了一忖，"没关系。五点不到我就会睡醒。"

"你怎么知道你会？"

"行军习惯了。"

"如果打起来，你就要走了。"她本来不想说这话。

"我会找个人照应你的。"

"你睡觉时把手放在这儿吗？"

"小时候会。放在那里似乎最安全，不知为什么。"

"我也一样，但老妈子总是拉开我的手，就不再放了。"

但是他的手夹在她腿间，似乎像插进口袋里那么自然。他一个吻弄醒了她。周围灰茫茫一片。

"不不，你不是要走了么？"她叫喊，他已经一条腿压向她，身子滑上来。

有一会儿并不痛。海上的波涛在轻柔地摇晃她，依然是半梦半醒。他们的船已经出海，尽是诡异的一大片灰蒙蒙。然而他们浑浊的脸发出一股有安全感的气味，令他们想起床上的一夜眠。

他穿衣的时候她坐了起来，摸一摸他的肩膀、背脊与肘弯。

"别起床，那仆人可以领我出去。"

"不要穿鞋。"

他略一踌躇，显然是爱面子，"不要紧的。"

她听见他走在过道石板地的脚步声，一路清晰刺耳。她心里发冷，很清楚事到如今洪姨娘一定是知道了。但还是照样理好床铺，烧蚊香的锡碟里的烟蒂也一个个拣了出来，洗脸时趁机把那条藏着的毛巾也洗了。毛巾浸在热水盆里，隐隐闻见一股米汤的气味，这粥水也被视为生命的源泉。

六

"现在外边乱得很,"洪姨娘私下里透露,"你爹去发起了一个地方保安会,跟清朝倒掉的时候一样。但是现在不比当年了,那时候老帅只是他手下一员部将。这回老帅一定点过头,你爹断不会自作主张的。"

四小姐知道她话锋所向。

"他们家的老大算是好的了,没被宠坏。他媳妇是配不上他,但朱三小姐的事都传成那样子,他到底没让她进门。那就有些意思了。"

提起朱三,四小姐仍旧不动声色,继续拨弄手里的九连环。

"其实像他们这样的人家,娶两个媳妇平起平坐的又有什么?老师也许不肯让年青人娶两房,但也许是顾到朱家的名誉。除非是另一种姑娘,出身不一样的人家。姑娘家最要紧的是名誉。外边的人,抓住一点点话柄就讲得满城风雨。就拿你爹说,尤其是他现在又出山了，尽管大家都知道他跟陈家是老交情，他至少也不想显得自己听命于人。要是人家说他为了讨好姓陈的什么都肯呢？你知道你爹的脾气。就连老帅也不会插手——说到底是当爹的处罚儿女。还不要说我，我自己也会落下罪名。也不用我叨念，你自己心里头都有数。"

她自己为此而死也愿意，但是洪姨娘和老妈子怎么办？她们是她的地狱。只是她对地狱没有执念。眼前她不必言语，低着头就是了。洪姨娘的反应已是极度温和。尽管如此，他与她的事旁人只要一提就是亵渎，令她不由得绷紧了脸退缩。旁人看上一眼便已是误解。

洪姨娘没有再说什么。当务之急是阻止他又一次登门。他没再来。

事关自尊，四小姐不去问他将来。他不提，不表示他忘了。如果他试过跟父亲谈而因此受辱，他也不会愿意告诉她。东北的叛变之后，他长跪了一日乞求父亲的宽宥，这就从来没有告诉她。她是在一个亲戚家里听说的。

她一见到他便不担心了，什么事都像对镜微笑一样明晰。只是每次他去打仗，两人一别数月的时候，她才开始忧虑自己的处境。她想去他家里看看五老姨太以及他的孩子们，甚至于他的妻。他们是她唯一的亲人，她在自己家里只与陌生人同住。五老姨太常说起他的童年：

"他喜欢守在院子里一个池塘边上，等穿着新衣裳的人洋洋得意走过来，就扔一块大石头到水里，溅别人一身的水，自己拍着手笑。人家多窘呀，只好说：'少帅怕人是吧？'嘻哟，那顽皮劲儿。他长大一些的时候我成天提心吊胆的，怕在他父亲跟前没法交代。"她耷拉着膨松的眼皮，语气骄傲。

五老姨太全靠他才有如今的地位。她从前是小县城的一个妓女。如果他战死了，四小姐能想像自己如何投奔五老姨太，抱着她的膝盖跪地哭泣，恳求收留，说着这种场合的套语："我生是他家的人，死是他家的鬼。"少女去给情人送葬，一身素服：

　　　　白绸衫儿，白绸裙儿，
　　　　黑头发扎了白绸手巾儿。

这叫做望门寡：未婚夫死了而少女希望为他守节。在那关系松散的大家庭里，有他待如生母的老姨太，有他待如妻子的半老妇人，如果多加上一个她呢？她们不会拒绝？她太年青了，还不知道自己的心志，最终会改嫁，败坏他们家声。平常不过的说辞。自会有人押送她回到自己家，她父亲羞怒之下会杀了她。

阴历年之前他打来电话，"是我。我回来了。"

一听见他的声音她就仿佛霎时往后靠在实心墙壁上，其实她还手握话筒，动也没动。汽车开过来接她。

"回来了？"洪姨娘说。

"嗯。"

现在能用电话约定幽期，才不枉洪姨娘当初为了装私房电话而引起的麻烦与猜疑。洪姨娘的沉默使她一阵愧疚。那老妈子如今则是终日潜行，仿佛怀着鬼胎，随时要生出一个什么妖怪来。

长久围攻以后，他打赢了南口之战。他在前线一度患上痢疾，听人建议拿鸦片作为特效药，有了瘾。

"休养好了就请个大夫来帮我戒了。"

他不愿意让她看见他躺下抽大烟，双唇环扣粗厚的烟嘴，像个微突的鸟喙。鸦片就如堂子里的女人，是他父辈的恶习，两者都有老人的口涎味。

"想我了么？"他一只胳臂搂住她，探身过来看她别过一旁的脸。问题仿佛有性的意味，"想我了么？"

她终于僵着脖子不大由衷地点了点头。

"我嘴上有没有那个味儿？"

"没有。"不过是一种让人联想起老人的隐约的气味。在她心目中，鸦片是长者的一种残疾。然而战争没有给他别的还算侥幸。

"朱三小姐要嫁人了。"

"哦？嫁谁？"

他咕哝了一个人名。

"是做什么的？"

"政客。她可以嫁得再好些。"

他们谈到别处去了。忽然她向着他咧嘴一笑，脱口道："我真高兴。"

"我早就知道你憋不住要说了。"他半笑半嗔，而且似乎厌恨她环抱着的抚慰的手臂。

次日晚上八点后他打来电话，"是我。我今年想再见你一次。"

她也立即想到不然就是隔了一年才见面。"今天太晚了。"

"明天是除夕。"

"算了，不行的。"

"说是看戏好了。车子马上来。"

"好吧。"

"我跟他们看戏去。"她向洪姨娘咕哝一句。

"啧！马上就过年了，各有各忙，哪有这时候还周围逛的。你爹一定要说了。"她声音很轻却语带威严，简直是他在说。

默然片刻，洪姨娘转身向老妈子，快速地喃喃吩咐："到前头去说一声，帅府来接四小姐看戏去。"

老妈子走了。

"好了，还不赶紧收拾收拾——前头没说什么才好，但你也不能这个样子出门。"

他们真的去看了一场电影。从此他常带她出去看戏，在有舞会的饭店吃饭。要么他是逐渐豁出去了，要么就是非要逼出个结果来。他的医生每次都跟着来给他打戒烟针。她把头发盘起，以显得好像剪短了，身上的新旗袍与高跟鞋平时存放在他们幽会的房子里。人人都议论他们，但是她丝毫不在乎，不像在洪姨娘面前。人言只是群众的私语，灯光与音乐的一部分。她没机会听见老帅的话：

"他讨小找谁不行，偏偏是我老朋友的女儿。我成什么人了？就算他没有娶亲也绝对不能结婚。我们陈家没有先上床后进门的媳妇。"

她父亲走了他的第一步棋。

他把她唤到跟前，说道："我和北京大学的校长谈过了，他答应让你入学做旁听生。看看一两年内能不能把功课赶上去吧。"

没说为什么兄弟姊妹里独独让她进学堂。就当是时代在变，女大学生的婚姻前途有时候比较看好。实际上，上学给了她自由，一整天都可以自己安排。如果她堕落了，那是现代教育有问题，现成的替罪羊。不加管束任她撒野，总也强于由人非议她父亲把她给了陈家做小。两家之间未曾言明的紧张关系至此缓和。倘若事情吹了也许还是可以嫁掉她。朱三小姐不是嫁了？

洪姨娘赢得奇异的胜利，四小姐平生第一次见她精神振奋。忍受了这些年的忽略与轻视，她终于都报了仇。那男人怕了。她的孩子有靠山，他认了下风。四小姐前所未有地成了她的亲女儿。她尽情吐出心中的忧虑：

"现在时世还不太平，你最好自己做好打算，不要一味拖延。老帅因为他对唐家人的感情，肯定是为难的。可你也不去争那个虚名嘛。看在你爹份上，他总也不会亏待你。关键是少帅要找到合适的人跟他父亲谈，一个说得上话的人。全靠你自己拿定主意了。男人向来是不急的。"她微笑轻声说着，对于提起她青楼时代的阅人经验感到迟疑，也当心不要暗示他或许和别人一样没长性。"我不过是旁观者提醒你一句，看得出你也不是个没主见的人。人家会怪我为什么早先不说你。说了又有什么用。母女一场，徒然伤感情。"

四小姐仍旧默然。到了这时候，从前什么都不告诉她是无礼又伤人。但是怎么对她说他们俩从来不谈这些？

"朱三小姐嫁了人，还给丈夫谋了个官职呢。你们摩登的人也无非是这样。"

她对朱三小姐的婚事一声不吭，洪姨娘似乎特别佩服。现在是因为觉得她冷漠才爱她，这让她有点不安。

北京照常庆祝中秋节，尽管正跟北伐的广州政权——途中已分裂为南京和汉口两个政府——交战。他早早经去了河南前线，但是这天依旧是她一生最快乐的中秋节。她请了一个孤身留在北京的女同学过来，其后陪她走回宿舍。家里的人力车落后几步跟着，累了可以随时上车。灰墙灰瓦的矮房子使马路更显宽阔。远处劈里啪啦放着鞭炮，附近也偶尔嘭的一声空洞地炸响，吓人一跳。商店都上了排门，人人回家吃团圆饭去了。长街一直伸向那灰蓝的天空，天上挂着一个冰轮似的月亮。一说话风就把面纱往她嘴里吹。她披着每个女大学生都有的那种深红色绒线围巾，一路晃着给朋友带回去的那盒月饼。两人走在电车铁轨上，直到一辆电车冲她们直压过来，整座房子一样大，当当响着铃，听上去仿佛是"我找到的人最好，最好，最好，最好。"恰恰是她小时候一直想要的:站在舞台正前方，两只手攀着台板无论如何也靠得不够近。如今铙钹在她头顶上锵锵敲着。

次日他打电话来。原来前一天已经回来了。

"跟他太太过的中秋节。"洪姨娘哂笑一声，愤愤不平。

她只微笑。她自己也是要跟家里人吃团圆饭。

"梁大夫呢？"他让她在身边坐下的时候，她环顾了房间。

"那忘八羔子。被我撵走了。"

"怎么回事？"她从来没见他这样生气。

"他给我打的戒烟针是一种吗啡。"

"用吗啡戒鸦片？"

"他是故意的，好让我积重难返。"

"他到底是什么人？"

"我发现他是杨一鹏的人。"

她搜索脑中面目模糊的人名册。老帅最信任的那位副手？

"为什么？"

"他恨我。出了顾兴龄的事情以后，明摆着憎恨我。"

东北那场叛变。难道他是说他确曾参与？

"那次主要是要整掉他。"

矛头并不完全指向他父亲？罪行之大立即使她眩晕。造反的皇太子是什么下场？关押，赐死——面朝帝宫叩首谢恩，喝下毒酒自尽。无论他做了什么，那也表明他是男子汉，不仅是某人的儿子。也许她还有点悲哀，因为他做了不会为她而做的事。

"可他们说你——"她刹住了口。

"说我嫖妓赌钱昏了头，自己兵营里发生什么都不知道？"

"不过是说你大意了。"

"我还没那么傻。不错，我常跟姓顾的在兵营俱乐部打扑克牌。我们比较好的年青士官里他算一个。我们俩都想革新，但只要杨一鹏还在就没有机会。最后没有别的办法。倘若不是日本人插手就已经成功了。"

"他们为什么支持老帅？"

"他们不想俄国人在东北坐大。顾兴龄和基督将军结了盟，而他跟俄国人是一伙儿。"

她无法想像他站在基督将军那边反对他父亲。其后他在南口击败了冯以祥。今年两方又在河南对垒，这次冯属于南方阵营。

她的沉默使他多说了几句替他父亲辩护："有些人说老帅亲日。东北紧挨着高丽，他当然不能不敷衍日本人。但他总是这个态度：小事可以谈，大事一定拖。现在他连小事也拖，大事绝对免谈。甚至于为灭掉顾兴龄而定下的协议，他也从未执行。"

"顾后来怎样？"

"枪毙了。"

一时间两人都不做声。他能捡回一条命，是因为他是亲生儿子。

"你不能告诉老帅被骗的事？那些戒烟针。"

他略一摇头又半眨眼睛，表示绝无可能。但是同时会有别人向老帅告状，说他年纪轻轻成了瘾君子。

"前几天出了件好笑的事，可见我们周围这些人是个什么德性。有报告说南方军亵渎了首任大总统的坟，于是有人提议我们也要回敬，去污毁孙文的尸骸。"

"孙中山葬在这儿？"

"在西山。幸亏那天有个老国民党叶洛孚在场。他劝老帅说现在不兴干这种事了，而且首先要查清楚。查出来不是国民党，是基督将军的驻军干的。砍了树，房子也洗劫了，但是没有扰动墓里。叶就跟老帅说，既然孙文遗体正好在北京，我们应该加以保护，表示我们有器量。于是老帅派了一支小分队到碧云寺去。果然没两天寺里就来了几个带着锄头铲子的人，见这儿有兵驻守，徘徊了一阵子又跑了。"

"他们是谁？"

"齐永福的人。"

她猜度是首任大总统的旧部。

"我们也不算落后。国民党自己，两年前他们的右派斗不过左派，失势了，不惜大老远从广州跑到这边敌界来，在总理灵前开了个会，后来被人称作'西山会议派'。孙夫人自己——对遗体施行防腐永久保存，就是她的主意。"

"他还是生前的样子？"她叫道。

"嗯，她跟列宁学的，她亲共。当然她推在丈夫的头上，说他说过最好能保存遗体。孙的追随者很错愕。首先花费就非常大。最后苏联送了他们一副玻璃棺材。"

"她美不美？"

"眼睛很大。"

"是她还是她妹妹更美？"

"妹妹更活泼。孙夫人也活泼，只是他们刚来她丈夫就病倒了。他们在天津下船的时候，我代表老帅去迎接。我们到达北京那天下雪，从火车站坐汽车出来，除了欢迎团体还有大批的群众。大雪纷飞，屋顶上、树顶上全是人。"他近乎气愤地直冲着她说，"在天津群众也是一样多，只不过警察局长为了讨好段执政把他们赶散了。"

"孙中山真是那么伟大的人？"

"关键是他代表了共和的理想。辛亥革命时大多数人都不知道在发生什么事。可是到民国十三年，他们真的想要共和了。好比女人刚结婚的时候并不懂得怎么回事，后来才喜欢。你会吗？"

"不知道。我又没结婚。"话一出口她便懊悔，仿佛在提醒他。

"哦，'没结婚'。翅膀长硬了，呃？说说你是谁的人。"

"少来。"

"你是谁的人？说说。"

"少来。那一回孙夫人的妹妹也跟着他们？"

"没有，只是夫妇俩。他是应邀过来组织政府的。他的追随者满怀希望，觉得他会当选大总统。他一到便去拜访老帅，我也在场。寒暄过后，老帅马上站起来说：'我陈祖望是个粗人，坦白说一句，我是捧人的。今天我能捧姓段的，就可以捧姓孙的。我惟独反对共产。假如我们要搞共产，我陈祖望是宁可流血也不要赤化。'这几句话吹到老段耳朵里，他更是疑神疑鬼了。其实那一回才谈了半个钟点。孙文当然不承认亲共。可是有老段在，已经坐着那把交椅了。孙回到饭店，跟幕僚开会直到深夜，当晚就生病了。"

"他是这样死的！"

"病了几个月才去世的。老段一直没有去探望，葬礼也不出席，托词脚肿穿不上鞋。堂堂一国元首会没有鞋子穿！"

"至少他脱身了。"

"如今他正在看我们的笑话。他一下野政府就真空了。代理内阁有我们全部盟友的代表，当然维持不下去。内阁辞职以后，谁也不愿意就任。老帅很生气，说'随便找些人就行'。政府雇的人已经停薪半年了。逊帝溥仪仍旧每个月拿到三万块，是我们私人的钱。

皇权统治遗留下来的，就只有这份对所有上等人的尊敬。本来老百姓也不过是指望'豫人治豫''鲁人治鲁'而已。政府再不好，本省人总比外人强些。我们尽量由得各地自治。任何当地人只要有武装力量，足以把本土管起来，就能从我们这里得到一官半职。"

听上去形势很坏。"战争会不会打到这里？"

"战争的事难讲。论实力，我们没什么好怕。去年冯的部队在南口把战壕挖得很好，不过我们的加农炮火力也够猛，集中开火几天以后，地皮都掀翻了。广州原本是土枪土炮的革命党，现在有了苏联的军械和顾问，我们的盟友自然敌不过。像吴蟠湖，他接到自己前线快要溃散的报告，就派出大刀队砍杀逃兵。他的兵早已听说大刀队要来，向着火车窗里扫射他们。结果大刀队都不敢下火车。"

"这些盟友有什么用呢？"

"可不是，个个都只顾自己。吴挨打的时候，东南那边方申荃按兵不动，尽管他本来可以轻易切断南方军的补给线。轮到他吃了败仗，就贿赂长腿给了他去奉天的安全路条，亲自过来乞援，路上隐姓埋名穿便服，因为他一个败兵之将不配穿军装。老帅见他这样忍辱负重，就派长腿出兵帮他夺回了东南五省。"她听说过他们的长腿将军。"老帅就是那样。对敌人也识英雄重英雄,向来慷慨，给人留点面子。他最不能容忍的是以下犯上。所以长腿摽着老方奉承老帅，说服他自己出面做政府首脑。下属不算数，但同侪的支持……"

"他当上了大总统？"她嗫嚅道。

"没有，不是总统总理，只称大元帅。这是老帅谦抑的行事做派，一辈子只喜欢从旁辅佐。这样已经是破例了。"

他突然顿住了。她也听说过那句俗语"变古乱常，不死则亡"。年纪大的人改变习惯是个坏兆头。

"南边也乱糟糟的。"她说。

"他们有自己一套搞法。"

"他们是共产党？"

"不再是了。南京跟英美搭上线，甩掉苏联了。现在苏联希望我们来遏制南方。老帅不卖帐，下令搜查了苏联大使馆，把他们搞颠覆的密件都公布了出来。这方面他们不遗余力，有一段时间似乎他们就要在中国实现赤化了。"

"在南边？"

"在南方军所到之处。集会斗争地主，分田，把男装裁短——长衫是上等阶级的标志。而且攻击教堂和教团，仿佛是义和拳的重演。洋人确实招人厌恨，因为政府待他们总是一副奴才嘴脸，替他们说话，跟从前没分别。传教师在农村势力很大。排外一直盛行，共产主义便打着这个旗号渗透。老百姓心里有不平，给他们随便一个出口都会发泄的。不过共产党正在遭到清洗，他们不比义和拳长久。"

"孙夫人的妹妹现在结婚了吗？"

他微微一笑，"不知道，没听说。"

"她多大了？"

"跟我差不多大。"

"她不会已经二十七了吧？"

"我不知道，她自己没讲过。洋化的女人不提自己年龄的。"

"她总不能永远不结婚吧？"

"这些基督教徒说不准。"

"不是因为你？"

"不，不会。"

"她一定喜欢过你。"

"她正一心找个中国的领袖，恰好我有机会继承这个位子。"

"你说得她那样无情。"

"她自然是以她姐姐为榜样。"

"她非常美？"

"不是。"

"不，说老实话。"

"出洋念书的人别有一种清新可喜的气质，况且她也没有沾上一身男子气回来，叫人讨厌。"

"幸好老帅不会让你离婚。"

"哪里就到那一步了。"

"你不想娶她吗？"

"即使想过，我也是在大处着眼。男人也有希望跟某一家结亲的，好比一个亮灯的门廊，人人路过都看两眼，因为正好是你没有的东西。自从那一回群众在大雪里等候孙文，可以跟那样一个人发生的任何关系我都愿意发生。"

"但是你总要喜欢那姑娘。"

"那当然。我以前常想这些，不像现在，没有杂念了。"

"老帅知不知道？"

"他当成笑话儿——他儿子娶一个'吹鼓手'的女儿做媳妇！那是她父亲的外号儿，他从前在上海附近传教，弹簧风琴。"

这位社交新星，如今在她自己的往事中是一个亲切的人物。"不知道她为什么不结婚。"

"可能她也难。以她的年龄，即便是早几年，她遇见的男人应该都结了婚了。"

他拉了铃绳，从另一个院子叫来新雇的医生给他注射，与前任医生用的药剂一样。

他仍旧郁郁不舒，"咱们去趟西山吧。"

"这么晚，城门都要关了。"

"会给我们打开的。"

他们带着医生钻进汽车的时候，天已垂暮。从远处城门传来敲锣声，渐成悠长狂乱的呛——呛——呛——呛——呛——呛，警报着敌军来袭、火灾或洪水，世界的末日。汽车绕开了刚好赶上挤进城来的一辆辆骡车。一个警卫跳下汽车的踏脚板，喊叫着往前跑去。城门再次开启，铁灰色城墙矗立在黑色尘土上，汽车从当中的隧洞穿过。

长途行车，仿佛真把他们带到了他乡。抵达西山饭店后，他们却没有走进餐厅，免得碰见认识的人。只在金鱼池边徘徊，李医生进去代点汽水。她戴着墨镜，蒙着一层面纱。

"你像是个军阀的姨太太，到这儿来跟小旦幽会。"他说。

倒也没那么浪漫。他们在楼上套房与医生吃晚饭，谈到上午回去前要游览哪些地方，显然是要过夜。她可以说是同学家留宿，但是也怀疑自己太过分了。

野外寂静得不自然，这西式旅馆也一片死寂。北京城与它那守夜的钟鼓、市井的私语，都仿佛很远了。彻夜不归，又是在饭店里，她毫无羁束，以至于不再受法律的保护。她可笑地觉得自己是被抢来的新娘，落在一个陌生的村子里，终于受他支配。奇怪的是他看上去也忸怩，脱衣的时候不朝她看，带一丝微笑，眼睛很明亮。她想摆脱那异样之感，很快上床钻进被窝，他一上来就溜到他臂弯里。他却掀开被子，在灯光下慢慢检视她。

"你干什么？"

一只兽在吃她。她从自己竖起的大腿间看见他低俯的头，比例放大了，他的头发摩擦着她，使她毛骨悚然。他一轮急吻像花瓣似的向她内里的蓓蕾及其周边收拢，很难受。俘猎物的无奈与某种模糊的欲望在她内心轮流交替：要设法离开，不然就轮到她去吞噬他，拿他填满自己。她好几次试着起来。终究又还是他在上头向她微笑，脸泛微红。她让他来，近乎解脱般喘气，不断呷着甲板上摇晃的半杯酒。他一次次深扎进去，渐渐塞满她，忽然像鱼摆尾一样晃到一边，含笑望着她的脸。他停下来又看又摸。

"大了，呃？这个可不是长大了么？"

但是他们整夜都没怎么说话，不似往常。

七

父亲把她唤到书房去，用谈公事的口吻压低了声音说：

"现在时局紧张，老帅要把全家迁回奉天，今晚就启程。他叫你也一块儿去。也许最好是这种时候了——两家都省心。看在我们交谊的份上，他一定把你当亲生女儿看待的。不过，从今以后你也要学会做人了。现在全靠你自己了。让洪姨娘给你收拾行李，东西和佣人倒不必多带。想要什么晚些可以再送过去。就是要穿暖和点，关外冷。等时局平靖些你可以回来，你洪姨娘也可以去看你。"

她经历了一趟奇妙的旅程。专列上的陈家人把她当作来长住的外甥女那样招待。少帅夫人责不旁贷，亲自打点她的起居。她以后不再喊她大嫂了，改口叫大姊。关外是中国的北极，从前无数哀怨的公主与嫔妃出塞和亲，嫁给匈奴王。起伏不休的褐色山峦，横披着长城这条由成对的烽火台扣起的灰色带子，看得她惊喜不已。窗子里的景致永远一个样子，同一幅画屏不停地折叠开展，克喇嗑踢——克喇克！克喇嗑踢——克喇克！没完没了。

翌晨火车第一次停站，她望着停在旁边铁道上的一车兵。兵士们都站着，仿佛半身露出车外。一个农家子弟，双颊冻得红扑扑的，吃着大饼油条早餐。他瘦削的脸与脖子从棉制服里伸出来，就像揣在芝麻大饼里的油条末梢。他们在几尺之外说说笑笑，却听不见一点声音。她瞪大了眼睛，心口周围有种愉快的震颤；后来她觉得那便是预感。她到奉天的次日，老帅经同一路线返回时被人用炸药暗杀了。少帅的归途也有危险，但是他打扮成普通兵士乘坐运兵车，不坐车的路段则急行军，终于也安然到达。

正当局势一片混乱，众人又在筹备丧事的时候，他的出现仿佛是从天而降。听说他父亲最后一句话是"小六子回来了没有"，他哭了。他在族里排行第六。

他知道她在这里。留守北京，预备情势紧急便带她去东北的副官拍了电报到前线给他。

"爹在那样千头万绪的时候也想到了我们。"他对她说。

"他们说是日本人干的。"她说。

"十有八九。"他的眼睛在军帽的阴影下奇异地闪烁着——晚上他依然戴帽，遮掩因乔装剃光的头。

他历劫归来，这对于她是他们俩故事的一个恰当结局，从此两人幸福快乐地生活在一起。童话故事里往往是少年得志，这种结局自有几分道理。在那最敏感的年龄得到的，始终与你同在。只有这段时间，才可以让任何人经营出超凡的事物，而它们也将以其独有的方式跟生命一样持久。十七岁她便实现了不可能的事，她曾经想要的全都有了。除了据说是东方女性特有的娴静之外，如果所有的少妻都有某种自满的话，她则更甚，因为她比她知道的任何人都更年青，更幸福。一种不可动摇的笃定感注入了她的灵魂，如同第二条脊梁。她生命中再也不会有大事发生了。

"先前我们听说老帅已经动身回奉天，都觉得看情形是要撤退了。"他告诉她，"我们在那里扶乩玩儿，更深人静的，心想不如问问战事吧。乩仙在沙盘上批了'大帅归矣'，我笑了起来：'我们太神机妙算了，谁不知道大帅在回家路上？'当晚就接到了电报。"

火车是在皇姑屯的铁路桥上被炸毁的。

显然他在那故事中找到安慰。如果真有任何形式的鬼神，则他父亲可能仍在左近。他被各方敌友派来的吊客包围着：基督将军、国民党、日本人、山西王，在葬礼上全都各有说客，敦促他订约，结盟，承认政权。他对长腿将军关上了东北的门户，任他被人扫荡。他对东北的日本顾问停发津贴，又邀请 W. F. 罗纳前来。此人有临危仗义的名声。

"他们说这里枪毙了两个人。"她的老妈子悄声对她说。

"在哪儿？"

"办公楼那边。"

她稍后听说其中一个是杨一鹏，害他染上吗啡瘾的那个。晚上他进来更衣。

"哦，替我拿裤兜里的银元来。"

他喜欢把玩那枚钱币，还拿去镀了金。此时握在手中掂量着，面带微笑。

"昨晚杨何的事我拿不定主意,就掷了银元。"

"不!"她心中一沉。

"一直有人跟我说他们靠不住。""叛乱""政变"这些吓人的词极少直说。"可是也说不准。人总会妒忌,我和杨一鹏合不来又是尽人皆知的。现在不是记仇的时候。我最后告诉自己,正面逮捕,背面处决。三次作准。"

"全是背面?"

"三次都是。我怀疑这银元一面轻些,又试了三次,正面处决。而三次都是正面。"

递来的钱币上是首任大总统蓄胡髭的浑圆头像,她缩了缩。她不迷信,但是她信他。他很快把它放进口袋里,见不着了。

"我很难过,因为老帅的缘故。"

"现在他会明白的。"她说。

"他只跟杨见了一面就让他去开办兵工厂,那时杨刚从日本留学回来。老帅用人一向这样,不管是亲戚还是陌生人。"他提高声音,听起来因嗓门拉开而变尖,她不由得看了看他。他父亲识人有方,却从来不指望他,可见他不成器。起先她没悟到这一层,只是混混沌沌想起他父亲其他让他不以为然的亲信,比如长腿将军。

"那一回在南边打仗我和长腿住一个房间,只隔着一道帘子,"他曾经说,"他叫了三个女人,还不停问我,要一个吧?我只好拿毯子蒙头,假装睡着了。"

但是到了上海,他包下一个饭店房间,与长腿还有别的军官推牌九,无日无夜,一个多星期里倌人进进出出穿梭领赏。他们玩乐的那一套，他更在行，而他偏好的是他们碰不了的女人。

"有一回长腿为了个清倌人大闹了一场。临上前线，他从上海堂子里叫了个清倌人。用处女开苞交好运，跟用牺牲祭旗是一个道理。结果他没有'见红'，就要老鸨'见血'。其实谁敢要他？肯定是那姑娘已经跟人有染，不敢告诉老鸨罢了。"

然而长腿究竟是老帅那样的风云人物；他自己不过是儿子，虽然打了许多仗，却依然未经风浪。一向都有人确保他不会失败，或至少不会丢脸。

"我问杨何关于兵工厂和铁路的事。他们要先去核查。这一回我把他们叫到这儿来，他们还是含糊其辞。我走出房间。一分钟后，门打开，几个军官进来射倒了他们。"他小声说着，惊恐地微笑，"罗纳才听说了这事儿。他一定觉得他闯到贼窝来了。"

"你有没告诉他原因？"

"我把正面背面的事也说了。"

"那怎么行，人家会怎么想？"

"他见我比起在北京的时候变化那么大，想必早已大吃一惊了。"他看着镜中的自己。

"你瘦了。还没有从回来的那趟路缓过劲儿来。"

她像家里其他人一样，乐意将他的毒瘾看成是麻烦的小病——尽管偶有窃议，视为阿基琉斯之踵。只要父丧的危机一过，他就会有时间去医治了。目前压力还太大。

"像那些唱京戏的，"他说，"有点名气的角儿都抽大烟，不然应付不了紧张的生活。"

"也为了安抚他们的女戏迷嘛。"他有个朋友俏皮地说。

他笑了起来，"他们确实有这个问题。"

从前常有一帮年青人跟他一道骑马，都是些军官或大地主的儿子。如今他在清朝皇帝的北陵建了新别墅，邀他们过来开狩猎派对。四小姐喜欢北陵那些巨大的建筑，经满族人淡化的撒马尔罕风格相当简朴，被高大的松树林环抱着。别墅不过是一组红砖小房子。她听说这些聚会上有姑娘。他说那是他的坏名声招来的谣传。另一次则是打猎后赌钱，有几个人的太太也过来参加。某人的太太"盯得好紧"。两人都觉得非常可笑。

府里人仍旧叫她四小姐，但是外面现在都知道他有两个太太。大姊庆幸自己绝处逢生。假如四小姐不是已经来了，他父亲身故后他大概会想要离婚的。依现在的情形与时世，离婚肯定是不提了。三年守孝期也把婚庆排除在外——原本是个棘手难题。从简的摆酒请客又太像是纳妾。"过些时候再看看老帅的意思吧。"五老姨太曾经说。现在问题全解决了，只消在家里安安静静磕几个头。她地位平等，但于法律不合。

他们三人住在一个院子里。大姊说这样方便，他可以随时拿到衣服与物品，不必传送。仍想操持家事的妻子历来有这种安排的权利。她基本遂愿。另外两人太满足，没什么好挑剔。这府第是微缩版的北京故宫。穿过一道墙和假山花园，就是三层的办公楼，木雕花饰门楣，挂着老帅手书的一块横匾"天理人心"。花园门头上刻着另一句题铭"慎行"。周围是一溜仆役警卫住的房子，有手枪护卫队与汽车队。

"新房子盖好了咱们叫罗纳来一块儿住，"他说，"目前他还是待在饭店里舒适些。"

"他成家没有？"她说。

"结过一次婚。"

"在美国？"

"不是，这些年他从来没回去过。他们是在中国认识的，两人来自同一个州。他当时一定想家了。她嫌他太迷恋中国，走掉了。"

她笑起来，"只有外国女人才介意这样的事。"

"至少传说是那样的。他倒是出了名的正人君子。宋秘书把他比作孔夫子，周游列国，想找到一个君主来奉行他的治世之道。去年为了阻拦他南下，老赵专门成立了统计局，好让他痛痛快快地收集数目字。美国人相信数目字。他一个月有一千元经费。老赵说：'那罗纳真迂，一千块钱是给他的，没想到他当真雇人发薪水。'这还不算，北京陷落后他自掏腰包发工资。南京答应他会保留统计局，但是最终也没有把钱还他。"

她喜欢听他们谈话，给了她一种前所未有的感觉，仿佛坐在一个高高的亭子里，敞风向阳，眼光越过旷邈平原一直望到黄河。一切都在她面前，即使由于陌生的人名地名而模糊不清，更因罗纳不准确的发音愈加混乱。他也说到一些不可思议的事，包括他自己付钱给反对二十一条要求的抗议者。她在大学那年听说，那场示威游行是学生运动与民族觉醒的里程碑。但是她相信他，尽管她同时也有一丝怀疑与不忿，在他口中仿佛人人都是蠢材，比如他描述的孙中山：

"有个新闻记者问：'孙博士，您是社会主义者吗？'他转向我问：'我是吗？'我说：'你是国民党人所应是的一切。'"

"大博士现在终于隆重迁葬了，和明朝皇帝做邻居。"少帅道。

"葬在一个最浮夸的大糖糕里。有一万多人请愿，抗议为了开路运棺材上山而拆除他们的房子。"

"怎么遗体又不供瞻仰了？费了那么大的劲儿来保存。"

"他们跟共产党决裂了，不想仿效列宁。"

"你怎么看那个刚刚跟他成了连襟的继位人？现在他双手捧着神主牌了。"

她竖起耳朵。就是那个人娶了他的旧爱。

"我其实不怎么认识他，只是经他的连襟们介绍过。"

"他们是连襟政制。"

"法律上他真的离婚了吗？"难得一次开口，她谦谨地对着少帅问。他们依东方人待女性之道，这类交谈没有她的份。

"是的。"罗纳答道。

"乡下老婆好办。"少帅说。

"这桩事可不是把老婆搁在乡下那么简单。况且他不止于此，还改信了基督教。"

"他儿子声讨他是怎么回事？"

"那是他在他的亲俄时期送去苏联的儿子。俄国人总是叫儿子去声讨父亲。那小伙子是青年团的。中国共产党一份地下刊物登了他写给母亲的公开信，谴责他父亲背叛了革命。"

"还有，把劝他不要逛堂子的母亲踢下了楼梯。"少帅嘿嘿笑着说。

"那是他在上海经商时的事。"

"是他离掉的那个太太吗？"她问。她见过素瑚小姐与他订婚的照片，褶纹的雪纺纱裹着圆圆的肩膀，波浪烫发底下一张略大而柔和的脸，眉目含笑；他穿军装站在她身后，高瘦利落。她爱不爱他？她得到了她一直寻觅的——中国的领袖。而她是他自己挑选的，不是他依父母之命娶的那个女人。这就有极大的分别。

"他在证券交易所赚到一百万是真有其事？"

"崩盘的时候赔回去了。"

"那是足以刺激一个人参加革命的。"

"他早参加了，在陆军学校里。不过国民党在上海失败以后，许多人转入地下，有的就在交易所做事，在堂子里会面。他在那圈子似乎混得不错，待了十年。"

"他擅长一百八十度的倒转。"

"他把握住危机，乘势登上了极顶。问题在于一切都没有改变。旧势力集结起来，内战打不完。至今南京也做不出一件革新的事。我留下的时间不长，但也看清楚了他们在混日子。现在我不叫他们 Nationalists（国民党），改叫 Nationa-lusts（国贼党）。"

"嗯，一样的老中国。要是我们能杀掉几百万人就好了。也许那样我们就可以有作为。"

"那是布尔什维克的方法。"

"奏效就行。"

"那我不敢肯定。'大实验'已经进行了快十年，他们还是闹饥荒。军事上苏联谁也不怕它。"

"在这边它至少帮我们收回了汉口的外国租界。"

"租界其实最不必操心。只要全国其他地方够和平有序,也能吸引一样多的外国资金。你们各省连货币都没有统一。"

"要是我们可以把国家交给某个可靠的强国,托管个二十五年多好。"

"不幸无法办到。"

"我的大多数同胞会责怪我这样说,但他们没有试着立一番事业,或者说从来没有机会去试试。"

"我明白你为什么会有激进的名声了。"

"只不过是因为我父亲的地位,我讲话更自由而已。"

"我很高兴你不随大流,把一切归罪于外国人和不平等条约。其实中国需要更多的外国资本、更多的监督局,而非较少。虽然我作为区区一个新闻记者跟外国银行团斗过两次,我还是这样认为。"他随即讲起自己的故事,怎样施计让他们放弃了列为贷款担保的土地税。

"罗纳话很多,但是不该讲的事他绝对不讲。"一年多以后他告诉她,"他知道杨何的事情。他们曾经派人去上海见他,提出付两千英镑让他到伦敦洽谈,借款一千五百万英镑来开发东北。他说那是办不到的。他刚来这里的时候向那两人提起这事,他们很快岔开不谈了。他觉得奇怪,疑心他们是想用那笔钱搞政变。我处决了他们以后,如果他马上告诉我这件事,我一定受用极了,但是他什么都没说。他这人有担当。无论谁找他参谋他都保守秘密。"

"那你是怎么知道的？"

"他才说起来的，现在我们很熟了。"

罗纳说服他戒毒，又亲自打点他的膳食，推荐了几样他自己最喜欢的保健食品。他可以几个钟头滔滔不绝，论证琼脂和麦麸哪一种更有益处。他让他减少派对，一同打高尔夫球、游泳、钓鱼，带他去远足，让他耗尽体力。有人担心山径上会有刺客埋伏。自从他承认南京是中央政府，日本关东军的将官们便扬言要"教训陈叔覃，他背叛了我们"。

她喜欢看见他们俩像男童军一样出行。但是他的健康恶化了，医生建议他闭关静养至少一个月。

"外面一定会传说我死了，"他立即说，"会发生叛乱，让日本人有机可乘。"

他再度依赖吗啡，"等我们有了合适的医院，我第一个去治疗。"

斥资兴建了一所大学、一个现代港口之后，医院的计划便无以为继了。移民从战乱频仍的北方与中原涌来。最近一场战争规模空前，双方各有五十万人上战场，牺牲三十万人。无论是南京政府、基督将军还是和他结盟的山西王，都敦促少帅加入他们的阵营。他申明反对内战的立场，但是他们锲而不舍。

午餐时她听见罗纳说："至今没有人去碰。惟独这件事体现出中国国民的一致性。"竟是焦虑的声口。

"中国人只是把它看成不平等条约的一部分。"他说。

"如果他们托词于海关自主权而夺走海关，为什么安置一个英国人做税务司？把一个英国人换成另一个，这我不能理解。"

"老殷在山西孵豆芽太久了，办外交没有经验。"

"还偏偏选中贵甫森－甘这么一个人。"

"他够没良心嘛。又是名作家。"

"所以他不怕来到这帮演闹剧的军阀中间做随便什么事。饶有趣味，写写又是一本书了。"

他们打高尔夫球去了。她随后便听说，"我们要参战了。"

她以为早有共识，他要尽可能长久地保持中立。

"条件必须是国民党清理门户，开放政府。"罗纳先前说过，"空头支票不算数。"

她不希望他去打仗，所以熟知反对的各种理由：留下半空的东北，日本人会趁虚而入。东三省比中国其他地区都更工业化。国民政府的代表乘车参观兵工厂，三个钟点才走毕全程，振奋不已。东北地大物博，开发它，就比插手内战更有利可图。算起总账来，老帅那些战争是得不偿失的。

"所以你这里也有孤立主义者。"罗纳曾经说。

"罗纳为什么那样讨厌那英国人？"她问。

"哦，贵甫森－甘。待在中国的外国人里面他是一种典型，一心想着多捞好处。罗纳自己对钱向来很有原则。"

"他们认识很久了？"也许做妻子的往往疑心丈夫的至交在利用他。她感到愧疚不安。

"对，在北京。贵甫森－甘写了许多关于中国的书，据说很精彩。罗纳也写东西。"

"文人相轻，自古而然。"她笑着引用古语。

"这是几时的话？"

"不知道。也许是魏晋时候的吧。"

即将降临的考验沉重地笼罩着他们。他要投身于新闻报上所谓的中原大战、问鼎之争。日本人支持另一方。她从不希望让他经受任何考验，因为这些都不公正。老话是不以成败论英雄。

他入了关。在北京找到公馆后，立刻如约让她和大姊一道过去。他不住大帅府，防止别人将他与旧政权混为一谈。东北人这次是以和平之师前来。他的大军一压境，仗便打完了。

关于这次行军，他津津乐道的是贵甫森－甘的故事。

"他写信到司令部给我，答应送来两百万现款，此后每个月一百万，条件是我让海关保持独立。我叫他过来面谈。

"罗纳问：'你为什么这样做？'

"'我想看一个英国人丢脸。'

"'小心点。大家会认为你们只是谈不拢。'

"'你在场做证人好了。'

"'我不知道。他会认为你感兴趣的。万一你们谈得成什么，你会多了一个朋友而又少了另一个。因为我只好离开你了。'"

罗纳先前也一度这样威胁。他在奉天遇见一个老相识，是英国的从男爵，曾经在印度的公职机构做事，后来在公使馆任职。

"你在这边做什么？"罗纳问。

"少帅请我来做他的顾问。"

在家晚饭时少帅宣布："罗纳丢下了乌纱帽。妒忌得跟女人似的。"

"什么妒忌得跟女人似的，"大姊说，"你扪着胸口问问自己的良心。"

"于是贵甫森－甘到司令部来了。他说：'你一定得让我官复原职。'

"我问为什么?

"'因为我们合作可以赚大钱。'

"'你是指从海关抢钱。'

"'倘若你不帮我，我不知道该怎么办。'

"'问殷锡三去。'

"'他跑了。'

"'那你也跑呗。'

"'给我一个礼拜行不行?'

"'为什么?'

"'我要关照我雇用的人。'

"'给你一个礼拜榨干海关! 我限你一天之内把它还给接收机构。'

"他匆匆忙忙走了。两天以后他的一个雇员因为分赃纠纷枪杀了他。天晓得一个外国人要在中国横死有多难。他大概是义和拳以来第一个死于非命的外国平民。英国终于不派军舰干涉了。"

在难以置信的胜利之后，最初的日子如在云雾，就只有这故事令她觉得那是真的。贵甫森－甘可谓那场战争唯一的牺牲者。三十万无名死者是他参战前的事。山西的殷氏到大连暂避，后来仍旧回去做一省之王。基督将军下了野，带着老婆和精兵躲到山东一座风光旖旎的山上。南京并不追究到底；全国通缉他们已是足够的惩罚。要不是那英国人死了，一切都会惘惘如梦，仿佛一场枕头大战，线头裂开，拍打出毛茸茸的云雾。她感到司令部的那场会谈是他人生的第一个高峰。他终于证明了自己，还是在罗纳面前，而罗纳就是全世界。

"有一件怪事，"罗纳道，"从他第一本书上，能看出拳民之乱给他最深印象的是抢掠。想不到他三十年后为此丧命。"

"《北京实录》。"她说。

"嗯，很好的第一手记述，垂涎的模样跃然纸上。"

"他还写过一个短篇小说叫《抢掠》。"

"哦？讲什么的？"

"同样的故事。"

"英国人、印度人和哥萨克人抢掠皇宫？"

"嗯，他八年后把它重新写成一个短篇。"

"活见鬼了。"

"原来你也看他的书。"少帅得意地说。

"我也好奇嘛。那时候你们都在讲他。"

他喜欢在罗纳面前炫示她，但她通常不说话。罗纳待她也谨慎规矩，较少注意她，不比对待帅府里的未婚女孩子。他平素喜欢跟少女打趣，得是会说英文的才行。然而一个男人有两个太太，不管他们看上去多么摩登，还是视为守旧派更安全。

"他始终在给他们找藉口，"罗纳道，"他们是德瑞克的海盗团伙，从劫掠者手里劫财。满族自己则是从明朝皇帝那里劫来的。至于外国人掌管的海关，他们的财富是帝国主义掠夺的果实，虽然这话对于他也许太布尔什维克了些。"

"这么说他只是按照自己一贯的信念做的了。"少帅道。

"作家是不该这样的。吠犬不噬嘛。"

他受任全国陆海空军副总司令，与罗纳一起坐飞机到南京出席国民会议。风传他回不来了。南京会留着他，再不然他父亲的老部下也会接管东北。他两个月后返回。他已结束了军阀时代。下一次南行，太太们也与他同坐一架私家飞机。终于是二十世纪了，迟到三十年而他还带着两个太太，但是他进来了。中国进来了。

The Young Marshal

by Eileen Chang

1

At the house party all the girls came out on the veranda to look at the street. A man down below tossed up a sheet of paper folded into a twin-hearts knot. They picked it up, untwisted it and read:

"Young lady, wait for me this time tomorrow."

They rushed indoors in a body. They were the first generation with unbound feet. Even in satin slippers the new "big feet" made them seem like a boisterous crowd.

"This must be for you." They passed the slip of paper around.

"Says who? More likely for you."

"Why me of all people?"

"Who told you to be so pretty?"

"Me pretty! That's you yourself. I never even saw what sort of a person it was."

"And who did? I had no idea what happened when everybody started running."

The fourth Miss Chou was too young to have to protest. She just grinned from under the bangs that blacked out the top half of her face. They stayed overnight. The next day at the same hour the girls said:

"See if the man is here again."

They hid behind a window and peered out, hippy with their posteriors thrust out in the figured satin trousers and their thick pigtail hanging down the cleavage. The young ones had two pigtails. But most were eighteen, nineteen and engaged to be married. They were so excited over this it was plain that they had never been in love. Fourth Miss was a little ashamed of the way they kept watch all afternoon. The man never came.

She herself had been in love a long time. She went to the Marshal's House on all birthdays and festivals. There it was always somebody's birthday, either the Old Marshal's or one of the concubines', not the sons' as it was bad taste to celebrate a youngster's birthday with three days' feasting and command performance by all the best-known actors. The Chous were invited on the "central" day so there was no danger of their running into more rowdy elements like the army officers. The eldest son of the house was an officer himself. Sometimes he appeared in a long gown, sometimes a western suit but she liked him best in uniform. Men's gowns were considered decadent and western clothes foppish, or like a compradore. A military uniform was both modern and patriotic. Soldiers were different, they were strong-armed beggars. The officers were feared in a different way. They had all the real power. When they happened to be young and mannerly they seemed to be the country's only hope. The Young Marshal as everybody called him was very handsome. When he laughed he had a sarcastic look, even with children. They followed him around. He carried on a conversation on a dead telephone for their benefit. She could not stand up for laughing. Once she went to watch the singers make up for their roles. An actor was using his study as a retiring room but the actor was on.

"Why don't you cut your hair?" he asked. "Why these pigtails? We're a republic now."

He chased her around the room with a pair of scissors. She was laughing until he held out a bushy black bunch to her.

"Here, you want to keep this?"

She burst out crying. At home they would scold and what would Father say? But it was only a false beard.

She had seen many private performances at relatives', in her own house too. Unlike the musty theaters these were in a courtyard under a roof of fresh matting casting a summery shade. The new stage lit by blue-white gas lights and the hubbub of a holiday crowd totally transformed home life. The feeling that something wonderful was going on that she did not quite catch drove her to go in front, see better, somehow protrude herself, get hit on the head by the shattering gongs and cymbals. She would put her hands on the stage boards and stare upward. The heroine stood right above her piping her song, plucking her own sleeve showing off the flowing white cuff. Her headdress of black-ringed brilliants flashed blue. Two long slabs of rouge from eyelid to jaw marked off a narrow white nose. The warrior's painted face loomed large as a devil's mask. His singing also came out in a bottled boom as if from behind a clay mask. A kick and leap flung up dust that Fourth Miss could smell, stinking slightly of horse dung. There was still something she was missing. She circled the three sides of the stage hand over hand. Those sitting in the front row reached out to protect their glasses of jasmine tea placed between the footlights. At the theaters she had seen people ushered onstage out of the wings in the middle of a performance and chairs set out for them in a row. They were important people with their family and concubines. It was said to be vulgar showing off but she envied them up there in the midst of things although it was doubtful they could see more from behind the actors.

That was when she was little. In the days of Wu Pan-hu as they say. Before that was Tuan Ching-lai's time. "Now it's Fung Yih-shiang." "In the south it's Fang Shen-chuen." Even the amahs knew the war lords by name. They may not know who the president was but they always knew who was actually in charge, and called him by his name, the one curious instance of democracy in a nominal republic. The Old Marshal was the only exception in this house because of his special connection with the master. Fourth Miss was hazy about their reigns and change-overs. A combination of snobbery and caution kept the wars out of polite conversation and reduced them to the level of city crime talks, a matter of staying in and watching the doors. "There's fighting outside. Nobody goes out," She would hear along with the boom of distant guns. The resident tutor taught as usual but the Englishwoman would not come for the girls'

English lessons.

"Phoebe Chou, 1925," the teacher had dictated the line on the flyleaves of all her books. The name Phoebe was just for the teacher's convenience. Her other given name was also not known outside the schoolroom. Her father was supposed to use it but he seldom had occasion to address her. She was just called Fourth Miss.

The Old Marshal coming inside the Pass last year had rented the former palace of a Manchu prince. The parties on its huge grounds were as big as a fair, acrobats and minstrels under the mat awning, Peking opera in the big parlor, another performance for the ladies in the second parlor, mahjong in every other courtyard, fireworks after midnight. She drifted around with big red bows on her pigtails, her long gown a stiff trapezoid. Wide sleeves jutted out flat and triangular above the wrists that dangled foolishly by her sides. People said the Young Marshal was sweet on the Chu sisters and often took them out dancing, of which he was very fond. She wished he was married to the Third Miss Chu, the most beautiful girl she had ever seen. His wife was homely and silent, four years older than him and seeming much older still. Fortunately she seldom saw them together. The rules of the day did not call for it. They had two children. She was the daughter of a war lord in Szechuan who had saved the Old Marshal's life once. In gratitude he married his son to his benefactor's daughter. To Fourth Miss it was one more thing to admire in the Young Marshal, to have paid his father's debt with his own life, so to speak.

She never heard the Chu sisters mentioned at home without a snicker.

"Running wild and their father lets them. Once the bad name is out even the youngest will suffer by it. 'Ha, the famous Chu sisters' people will say."

The Fourth Miss Chou did not have to be warned off them. She felt like a country cousin. Even the Fifth Chu ignored her except this one time when she asked, "Have you seen the Young Marshal?"

"No."

"Go look for him."

"What for?"

"Tell him somebody is looking for him."

"Who?"

"Not me anyway."

"Can't you go yourself?"

"I can't. It's all right for you."

"You're not much older."

"I look older."

"How should I know where to look? And just to tell him something without head or tail."

"Little devil. People seldom ask you anything and you put on airs." The Fifth Chu hit her laughing.

She hit back and ran. "You want to go, go yourself."

Rushing out of the crowd she went straight to look for the Young Marshal. Once out among the men she had to watch out for her father and half brothers, keep close to the wall, run for cover behind potted flowers, wander around the corridor walks pretending she did not quite know where she was. Fruit blossoms appeared in pale masses where the lights touched them in the courtyards. Servants bearing dishes went in and out the curtained doorways. A hubbub everywhere and music instruments being tuned. She was a tree growing toward a lighted window all her life, at last tall enough to peer in.

2

"Oh, is he in Peking? The Old Marshal seen him?"

"I haven't heard."

"He works through Old Fu."

"Is there talk that Old Fu has hitched a thread on the southwest?"

"Is that so. Hardly worth his while, what?"

"That's it. Canton will never amount to anything."

"Canton has gone Red."

"The Russians are getting out of hand."

"Hey, tonight we speak only of the wind and moon."

"All right, you there! You took in a pet without feasting us, now say how you should be punished."

"Ha ha! How did you get to hear? I didn't dare disturb you all for such a trifling matter."

"Punish! Punish!"

"Stand dinner! Make your honorable pet fill our cups."

Sharkfins were served.

"Chin chin! Chin chin!" And "Ai, ai—ai, ai—" little cries of warning with a hand covering the wine cup to stop it from being refilled.

There was an alternative ten-course western dinner for foreigners but W. F. Ronald brought a loaf of bread just in case. He was well-known enough to indulge in this one small eccentricity. He was no bigger than the Chinese but well-built, with an ordinary pleasant face, hair combed straight back, a high nose pointing straight out with two wry lines at the base. He reached for his glass of water.

"There is foreign wine." The Young Marshal signalled a servant. "Whiskey? Champagne?"

"No, thanks. I don't drink."

"Mr. Ron never drinks, not a drop, heh heh heh!" the Minister of Education explained laughing.

"America prohibits wine," said the Under Secretary of Navy who had studied in the naval academy in England.

"Is pork also taboo?" another said.

"Actually a little port won't hurt. Very mild," said the another.

"You're not a Prohibitionist are you?" The English author Gravesend-Kemp pretended alarm.

"No."

"Then you must belong to one of your fascinating sects."

"Not used to Chinese food," observed another.

"Or Chinese women, heh heh heh! Mr. Ron is really a good man, no hobbies of any kind," said the Minister.

"Anyone who doesn't like Chinese women doesn't like women," Gravesend-Kemp said with a little bow.

"Eight Big Alleys don't represent Chinese women," the Young Marshal said.

"Hear, hear!" said the Under Secretary.

"Unfortunately they're the only ones a foreigner can get to know," Gravesend-Kemp said.

"What is this about?" Ronald gathered that it had to do with himself.

"Your manhood is being defended," said Bancroft, born in Shantung of missionary parents. The three foreigners were placed side by side to keep each other company.

"A good thing I don't speak the language," Ronald said.

"Hear no evil, speak no evil," the Young Marshal said.

"Not at all? After all these years?" said Bancroft.

"Not a word. I don't want to. It's just confusing."

"It may contradict your own ideas about China," Gravesend-Kemp said. The Englishman was a little high. His dark eyes were set close to the level black eyebrows. The lower part of his face was big, making him look fat. He was famous for his first book about the Boxers' Rebellion, which he had been here in time to see. Naturally he could not stand the American newspaper hack turned advisor to the Chinese like himself.

"It's just as well not to understand a lot of what you're being told," Ronald said, "when people are just being polite or trying to give a good impression."

"He's just a poor linguist masquerading as a cynic," Bancroft said.

"It is said that people of strong character have difficulty learning another language," the Young Marshal said.

"What about you? Would you call yourself a weak character?" said Gravesend-Kemp.

"Leave me out of this."

"Certainly a strong character, our Young Marshal," said

the Under Secretary, "pioneer in everything, poker instead of dominoes, movie actresses and society girls instead of singsong girls."

"Insulting our women again. That reminds me, when are we going to play poker?" he called across the table in Chinese.

The Minister shook his head and waved a hand. "In poker I dare not keep you company. The Ministry of Education is a poor organization."

"You're too modest."

"Hey, Young Marshal, a Shanghai newspaper elected the Four Princes of the Republic. You're one."

He sniffed. "Princes of the Republic. That's a good swear word."

"Who are the others?"

"There's Yuan Hun-chuang—"

All comments passed over the other two, mere war lords' sons, less flattering comparisons.

"Hun-chuang is a poet and calligrapher but no match for the Young Marshal in military matters and all round brilliance."

"He's selling calligraphy in Shanghai. A real bohemian."

"Half Korean, isn't he? His mother was one of the two imperial concubines from Korea."

"Were you here during the restoration?" Bancroft asked Ronald.

"Which one?"

"The first president turning emperor."

"As a matter of fact I started the whole business. It was at just such a dinner as this. I was saying it's still debatable whether China is best suited to a monarchy or republic. And that set all the Chinese talking at once. Never saw them so excited. Within weeks the so called 'Security Planning Society' sprang up all over the country boosting restoration."

He had fought the movement he touched off. He helped a dissident general under house arrest, smuggling him out of Peking in a laundry basket. The general stirred up other provinces against the new emperor. Ronald arranged for him to abdicate and continue as president. But the rebels insisted on retirement. Ronald had to quiet his fears for the safety of his family and ancestral graves before he would resign. Like a lonely champion Ronald had played both sides of the game.

"I say, are you from Texas?" Gravesend-Kemp said.

He smiled. "No, Oklahoma."

The Chinese listening to the translation nodded so steadily and heartily their heads made circles in the air. Contemporary history was unwritten and unsorted, a dangerous subject never to be committed to writing in their time. Truth has a thousand faces.

"Some has it that a singsong girl smuggled him out of Peking."

The Under Secretary added diplomatically to Ronald, "People knew somebody must have. It makes a better story if it was the girl he was going with."

"So I became a singsong girl."

"Tch, tch, how could you?" Gravesend-Kemp said.

"What's Hsu Chow-ting doing abroad?" Ronald asked the Minister.

"Borrowing money."

"For the usual purpose? Build up the army."

"Heh heh heh heh!" the Minister sounded slightly embarrassed. Hsu was the Premier's man. The Premier had no army and ought not to need any with two protectors, the Old Marshal and the Christian General.

Ronald returned to his cold steak. He had this trick of suddenly shooting out a question after one of his long stories. When a listener was lulled into a sense of security the natural desire to compete for attention was apt to surface and the answer was more likely to be truthful.

The Chinese seemed to be still talking about the restoration. There was that story about mine host and the restoration, of course Ronald would not tell it here. The Old Marshal was already the ranking officer in Manchuria at the time. Peking saw to it that he got a governor he got along with. This was one of the fourteen governors who had sent in secret petitions for restoration. As a result he was created duke, first class. The Old Marshal was viscount, second class. The Old Marshal was not pleased. He got up a large group of officers to go with him to the governor's house saying, "Your Excellency being kingmaker will want to attend the coronation. We're here to beg for instructions as to the date of starting, so we can prepare the send-off."

The governor could see that he had to go. "I leave for the capital tomorrow evening."

The Old Marshal played it out to the end, gathered all the staff for the farewell feast. Manchuria never had another governor. The new emperor had his hands full.

"He wanted to be emperor as far back as the Korean expedition," the Under Secretary translated. "He was taking a nap in his tent. An orderly came in and saw a huge frog in the bed, was so scared he broke a vase. He did not scold, just told the man not to talk. Dangerous if the Manchus knew one of their generals was going to be emperor one day."

"Is frog a royal emblem?" Gravesend-Kemp asked.

"No, any big animal. Turning into one when you are asleep is said to be a sign. What really happened must be the orderly was afraid to be punished for breaking a vase and so invented the excuse."

"A big frog," the murmur ran around the room. No one dared praise the orderly for a quick imagination. The first president had rather looked like one.

Just the sort of colorful superstition that would interest foreigners, Ronald thought. He had no patience for these things that supposedly make the Chinese different, because he knew they are not.

"I had this from Liu Tze-chien who was in his secretariat. He actually considered marrying a Korean princess to become king of Korea."

"He's from Honan, that's why. The seat of the earliest dynasties. The mind is influenced by the royal traditions. He'd never have dared if he was born south of the Yangtze," said a man from south of the Yangtze.

"He's a nineteenth century Chinese," Ronald said. "Very capable, but he aged early. Quite worn out in his fifties, hair and moustache all white. He got the idea that I'm for the Nationalists. Greeted me every time with '*Lao ming-dang*, old Nationalist, what's new in Canton?' "

"Mr. Ron has a bellyful of anecdotes," the Minister said and repeated it in English.

"What else is there?" Ronald said. "The last twenty years was just a jumble of personalities, the kind that figure in anecdotes."

"How old are you anyway?" the Young Marshal said.

"Oh, I saw you the other day," Ronald said.

"Where?"

"Playing golf on the Great Wall."

He laughed. "Very good golf links."

Quite a memorable figure in his wide white flannel trousers on the green grass of the inner slope. He was said to be fond of all things modern, had been close to the Y. M. C. A. people in Mukden while learning English. Talked better than he listened, got away the minute he sensed advices and lectures. The father was a sloe-eyed frail little man with a forced smile under the moustache. Ronald knew his type. In Oklahoma they had local big shots who had started life as cowboys like the Old Marshal. No, he was a horse doctor, to be exact. Manchuria seemed to have been very much like the Old West. Horses ploughed the land and were ridden across great distances. To avenge his father who was killed by a gambler he got into the enemy's house at night and shot a maid servant by mistake. He ran away to join the army. Years later he came back, was promptly arrested but escaped from prison. He hired himself out as protector to a village. It was difficult to tell between protectors and bandits, hence the legend that he had been a *hu fei*, bearded bandit, also called red beard, possibly originating from marauding white tribes on the Amur but more likely a reference to the standard make-up for robbers in Peking Opera. With a dozen men under him he settled down and sent for his wife. His son the present Young Marshal was born in a village. On being challenged by a large gang he proposed a duel with the leader who had no sooner said yes when the Old Marshal whipped out a pistol and shot him dead. So by a quick draw he won his first important battle and absorbed a hundred new men into his following.

The cowboy had grown old, smoked opium and kept many concubines. He had his own way of doing things. Ronald could always get a job here. The Minister of Education was an old acquaintance, a carry-over from former governments, and had made him offers. The fact was practically any foreigner who accosted a Chinese official would be given the title of advisor and 200 Yuan a month just to keep him quiet. It had been so since Manchu times. Of course advisors like Gravesend-Kemp were not after the 200 Yuan. The Old Marshal must have paid him a tidy sum for his latest book, "The Lonely Anti-Communist: His Struggles in Far Asia". Unlike his other works this one was published by a British bookstore in Shanghai. The Anti-Communist was the Old Marshal, the only bulwark against Communism in China. The western powers were urged to give him a free hand to take back from the Russians the Chinese-Eastern Railway in Manchuria. Japanese interest in Manchuria was scarcely mentioned. Did the Japanese commission the book? It was not like the Old Marshal anyway to place such trust in the powers of writing. Ronald made a mental note to find out.

He noticed the Young Marshal get up and leave the room, and suddenly felt empty. Had he talked to impress the Young Marshal? Partly it was because the dinner tonight so reminded him of the other on the eve of the restoration, the same big round table and buzz of talk, Tiffany lamps and an overall white glare, the room a rosewood cage, curlicue partitions with moon gates cut out of them, hung with apricot silk. That was already a dozen years ago when he was the youngest old China-hand. Sometimes he wondered why he stayed. What is he doing here, reporting on the murky political scene, telling stories at dinnertables, writing long letters on Chinese politics to his sisters in Coon Creek, Oklahoma. There is always a living for him here. The Chinese don't forget people easily. Has-beens are respectable here. There is something sinister about present power and wealth, especially now. The past even as recent as a decade ago has mellowed enough for nostalgia, as with the first president. Aside from being the granddaddy of war lords, the maker of things as is, he inherited the mantle of authority from the Manchus as their last chief official. Nevermind that he helped bring them down. That's the trend of the times and it is generally agreed that the Manchus are impossible. After he died his favorite pupils took turns succeeding him as president or premier. They constitute the only legitimate descent. Premier Tuan, the last of the star cadets of the military school he had founded, lost out to the new war lords risen from the ranks or worse. However all these upstarts have tried to maintain continuity by supporting one of the first president's men. The Old Marshal has got Tuan out of retirement to head his government, a sorry come-down for Tuan, everybody thinks.

"Hey, *lao ming-dang*!" what the first president had called him, being shouted across the table. The rest he did not understand.

"He said Old Nationalist, how is your fellow spy?"

"Who?"

"The Aunt of the Country."

"And who is that?"

"In Canton aren't they calling Sun Yatsun the Father of the Country? That makes his wife the Mother of the Country, and her sister will be the Aunt of the Country."

"Which sister?"

"The little one who is here as beauty bait. It looks like our Young Marshal has a mind to be the country's uncle by marriage."

"Not so loud," somebody cautioned.

"Gone. Off to the dance at Peking Hotel."

"So a north-south alliance is in the offing," another said.

"She will bring in more dowry than two battleships."

The Under Secretary of Navy had got the post by defecting

from Canton with two ships.

"What does the Old Marshal think?"

"Our Old Marshal is great on loyalty. With his feeling for his in-laws, divorce is out of the question."

"Better tell that to the lady."

The Under Secretary was told to translate to Ronald.

"I've scarcely seen her since she was a little girl."

"As old friend of the family it's your duty to tell them she may lose her virtue here and lose face for the late Dr. Sun."

The Young Marshal was in the courtyard talking to Fourth Miss.

"Who's looking for me?"

"Don't know."

"Don't run. Who made you come anyway?"

"Nobody made me. I come and go as I please."

"So where're you going now in such a hurry?"

"To the show."

"Which show? I'll go with you."

"People are waiting for you."

"Who?"

"Ask yourself."

"Little devil, so you won't tell, then I won't go."

"Then don't go, who cares?"

"You don't want me to."

"That's the thanks I get. Next time see who will take a message for you."

"What message?"

She struck him and they wrestled under the banana palm.

"Come-back-come-back, where're you off to?"

"To tell Big Sister-in-law."

Everybody knew he was not afraid of his wife. That wouldn't scare him. But she did not see him together with the Third Miss Chu later that evening and thought he did not come. Theirs was the rendezvous, in the courtyard just outside the roomful of liverish faces around the scarlet tablecloth, some standing up bellowing unsmiling, urging wine or declining it or challenging another to finger game, in the kind of male ceremoniousness that had always struck her as grotesque and completely incomprehensible, a circle of red cows being led through some temple ritual older than Confucius. The foreigners smiled fixedly, faded sepia heads resting on tall white collars like photographs. How like him to be with the foreigners instead of people like her father.

She could not get over how she had answered back. At

home she was very quiet. "Don't start anything" was Aunt Hung's constant admonition. Her mother was dead, she was brought up by another concubine. All the other children had backing while Aunt Hung had long been out of favor. He had also lost his mother early and had been reared by the Fifth Old Concubine.

"Those young masters of theirs, no law, no heaven, the minute their father's back is turned," Aunt Hung had said.

"Not like us here," the amah agreed.

"They don't go in for these things," Aunt Hung half winked.

They chatted about the old days, putting each other right. Fourth Miss discovered that her father had given the Old Marshal his start. As viceroy of Manchuria he had granted amnesty to the bandit leader and made him a captain. Came revolution, the viceroy's inclination was to save Manchuria for the Manchus. But there were revolutionist plants in the army. At a military conference an officer suggested that they follow the example of other provinces and declare themselves "sympathetic to the revolution" but retain the viceroy as military governor. The Old Marshal stood up and spoke out of turn:

"I Chan Tzu-wong don't sympathize with the revolution,"

and slapped his gun on the table.

After the conference which got nowhere the viceroy summoned Chan saying:

"The revolutionaries must be all set to act or they wouldn't have revealed themselves. I am ready to die for the emperor."

"Your Excellency need not worry. I Chan Tzu-wong happen to have a thing for loyalty. I'll be responsible for Your Excellency's safety."

He moved his own men in to guard Chou and ordered troops about in his name. The revolutionaries fled Manchuria. But Chou's plan to turn it over to Prince Su was foiled by the Japanese, possibly by the Old Marshal too. Chou finally gave up and took a job in Peking. As the governments rose and fell he retired. Now known as "king of the northeast" the Old Marshal pushed inside the Pass. The monster he had made had followed him to Peking although it was a grateful monster.

Fourth Miss was so surprised when she heard a half brother say, "We give Prince Su thirty thousand a year." Theirs was like a family of well-off pensioners, with enough to keep up the old rules but discountenanced by any new expenses. There was the great fuss when Aunt Hung put in a telephone in her courtyard so she could arrange to go out and play mahjong without using the family phone. She was paying for it herself, she had money of her own stowed away. The objection was that such extravagance might give rise to gossip. As if Aunt Hung could have a lover. Fourth Miss could not see her as a singsong girl. All that was known about her was that her last name was Hung before she entered the singsong house. Fourth Miss did not remember ever seeing her father in their courtyard. Aunt Hung had grown old quickly to save face, put on gold-rimmed spectacles and a black gown bulging in the middle from the fold of padded trousers.

"There's talk that Second Miss is engaged," an amah whispered and Aunt Hung whispered back:

"Which family?"

"The Tuans."

"Which branch?"

"Don't know. A widower they say. With lung trouble."

"These things are all in the stars. A healthy husband can also sicken."

"That's true."

"Any children?"

Fourth Miss heard them with consternation but never thought of it in terms of herself. Her half sister had always been a grown-up. The lottery of blind marriage gave everybody hope no matter what the odds were, especially when it was far in the future.

She learned this in the schoolroom:

"Slenderly swaying, just over thirteen,

A nutmeg on the bough in early March.

On three breezy miles of Yangchow road,

At all the windows with pearl blinds up

There's none as fair."

"Written for a courtesan," the tutor said.

It was inconceivable how the most beautiful courtesan of old Yangchow had been the same age as herself. Thirteen was actually twelve by modern reckoning which did not count you as a year old at birth. She felt the gulf of a thousand years looking across at the other thirteen-year-old.

3

She pestered a cousin to do her hair for her just for fun, curl the fringe with hot tongs and top it with a smoky rise. The pigtails were left untouched, tied for two inches with tightly wound pink silk thread. The mass of coarsened waves somehow set off the face and the lacquered plaits. She did not know whether she would be going to the Marshal's House the next day, one of the concubines' birthday. They may not celebrate this year. Both father and son were said to be in Mukden. She sat up all night sleeping face down in her arms on a table. The hair's slightly burnt smell excited her.

He was home. But as often happened at those circuses at the Chans' there came a point when the great day streamed by passing over her, smoothly bumpy, a big sun-warmed body of water, and there was nothing to do worthy of a day like this. She had seen all the operas. The best female impersonators did not come on till late. Nobody listened to the comedian waving his black fan with a patter of tributes to the birthday lady. She milled around with several other girls. A mound of potted peonies from Loyang, said to be watered with milk, was wired with colored electric bulbs leaving enough space inside for a table set for dinner. Today's magician was supposed to be good, a Japanese woman who had just played Shanghai. They talked about the programme in the Young Marshal's study. He had glanced at her curiously, then scarcely looked at her again. It was the hair-do. She steamed under the hot cloud of crimpy hair. She had not seen him for months. He no longer wanted to tease her now that she was older. The other girls, no Chus among them, did not have much to say either. He gave them knick-knacks some people brought him from Hangchow.

"Let's go. Time the magician is on," a girl said.

She was going with them when he said, "Here's a fan for you."

She opened the sandalwood fan and looked at it.

"A big young lady now. Won't speak to people any more."

"What?"

"So stylish too. Getting engaged."

"What nonsense is this?" She colored automatically. This was one thing he had never teased her about. Old ladies liked to do it.

"You won't tell. Won't invite me to the wedding either?"

"Stop that nonsense." It no longer sounded like a joke. The disaster suddenly lifted her up and put her among the adults.

"So? I'll be waiting for the feast."

"Pei!" she pretended to spit and turned to go. "What's the matter with you today?"

"All right. Sorry for being a busybody."

"Where did this talk come from?"

"Haven't you heard really?" For the first time she saw a gleam of anxiety in his eyes.

"There's no such thing."

"The Tangs are making a match for you."

"No such thing. I'll say no anyway."

He laughed. "What's the use of your saying no?"

"Kill me and I'll still say no." Here it came, the opportunity to die for him and to let him know.

"How about telling them the Fifth Old Concubine has

adopted you, so she will see to your marriage."

"I'm never going to marry."

"Why?"

"Don't want to."

"What do you want to do if you're going to be an old young lady all your life? Go to college? Go abroad? Go as my secretary, all right? What are you looking at?" He crowded close to see what she found so engrossing in the fan.

"I'm counting."

"Counting what?"

"The beauties."

He pointed to each painted figure in the garden and pavilions as he counted them. "Ten."

"Eleven."

"Ought to be twelve. It's usually twelve."

"I missed this one in the window. That's twelve."

"I got her. And here's one behind the tree."

"One, two, three, four..." She got ten.

Their nearness so confused them it came out different every time. Finally with an embarrassed little laugh he pounced on her, "Still another one here."

"Let me finish."

"What about this one here? So small we didn't see."

He did not let go of her wrist and held it up for examination. "Why so thin? You weren't like this before."

Immediately ashamed of not having turned out as pretty as she had promised to be, she mumbled, "It's only lately."

"Aren't you well?"

"Yes. I just can't eat."

"Why?"

She did not answer.

"Why?"

The more she kept her head down, the heavier it weighed, impossible to lift.

"Not because of me?"

He pushed up her bangs to see the hidden half of her face. She held still, nude and windblown. His arms were so loose around her it felt like a coat of powder. She struggled foggily. He must know too that it was no use. The difference in their age had him married long ago. They might as well have lived in different dynasties. She was free to love him as if she found him in a book. Otherwise how would she have been so shameless? Suddenly mortified, she did not know how to explain if he did not know. And how would he guess? Run and it would just seem like acting shy. She ran and heard the fan crunch underfoot.

Once out of the room she soon stopped running for fear of being seen. He was not following her. She was immensely relieved and happy. He loved her. Let them make their matches, it no longer matter what happened to her. He loved her, he always would. Surprisingly it was still afternoon. The clang of gongs came over faintly from the stage. She was so lonely she had to touch every pillar and post on the corridor walk. After taking another turn, definitely out of his sight, she skipped just to feel the familiar patter of pigtails on her shoulders, somehow as dim and far away as the sound of the gongs.

4

"Fifth Old Concubine of the Marshal's House has sent a car for Fourth Miss," the message came to her courtyard from her father's.

A man servant showed her to the Young Marshal's study. She stopped at the door smiling.

"Come in, come in. A good thing you came. Nothing to do today. Show you the tennis court. Just been put in. Do you play?"

"No."

"Ping pong surely."

"No."

The man would be back with tea. They sat waiting in

silence, he with bent head and a slight smile as if he was holding a cup of water he was afraid to spill.

The man finally came and was gone.

"I have news for you."

"I guess it was your trick."

"Sit over here. You don't want people to hear."

"Who wants to hear such nonsense?"

"Tch, people are worried for you. Did you hear anything?" She shook her head. "Good."

"You made it all up."

"Don't be without conscience. Do you know why nothing more was said? I had people drop a hint to the other side so they wouldn't go any further."

"What did you tell them?"

"That you're spoken for, what else?"

She beat him with fists. "Honest, what did you say?"

"Just that Fifth Old Concubine has a match in mind for you, only you're too young, it has to wait a few years."

"What if Father hears?"

"What of it? Nothing wrong with that."

"Maybe they won't let me come here any more."

"If you don't come I'll come to your house with a gun."

She wished she was locked up so he would come for her. "You're just fooling."

"No."

He pulled her to his lap where she sat with bowed head feeling his eyes glow beside her face like a jewel on her ear. He breathed her in. What if they could only have moments like this, she thought, it already seemed like a whole day. Time slowed down to eternity.

"Your eyebrows go like this," she traced them with a finger, then along the eyelids that fluttered down at her touch, and carefully down the center of the nose, checking each item to see what she had bought. He looked all new. Ownership made a difference, the way a picture card differed from a picture in a book.

"You haven't been to Peitaiho? Tsingtao is still better. We'll go. You learn to swim. If only I can have one night's sleep holding you like this."

Her smile stiffened slightly.

"Just hold you. Once when I was little I went out hunting and caught a deer. I wanted to take it home and keep it. We rolled over and over on the ground, I just will not let go. In the end I was so tired I just fell asleep. When I woke up it was gone."

She hugged him tight to squash the emptiness in his arms.

"It was quite big. Much bigger than I at the time."

"Did you have a gun?"

"No, I wasn't allowed to. Just bow and arrow and a knife."

"That was in Manchuria."

"Yes, it's good hunting country."

"Is it very cold?" Her mother had been a singsong girl there when her father was viceroy. Having been raised as her father's daughter only she never thought of herself as half Manchurian. Actually she looked rather like him with the same chiseled oval face and straight eyes. He drew away to look at her smiling.

"I'd eat you, but then there'd be no more."

"Somebody's coming." She heard a sound in the courtyard.

"Nobody comes here."

"All of us were here the other day."

"Nobody's let in when I'm here alone."

Alone with someone? Like the Third Miss Chu? It no longer mattered. They were the only two people in a cluttered world where she had to be careful not to step on all the chess figures and bric-a-brac scattered on the ground. She felt herself lumbering in sudden tallness.

"Young Marshal, topside calls," a voice shouted from down the corridor.

His father had visitors for him. He came back in nearly an hour to sit her on his knees again and stroke her ankle. At dusk he was called away once more. After a while the servant came to announce that the car would take her home.

The next time Fifth Old Concubine sent for her the car took her to a house she had never seen before in a long alley off a quiet street. The chauffeur held the door open. She hesitated and drew the head scarf over her face the way ladies kept out of the dust on ricksha rides. She went in with the filmy turquoise face past uniformed guards playing mahjong in a lighted room off the front court. He was waiting for her in the next courtyard.

"Whose house is this?"

"Mine. I have to have some place to go to. Never any peace in the house."

"I never knew you have your own house."

"I don't get to come here often. That's why it's in such a state. Come take a look around."

"Nobody else here?"

"No one."

It was like playing house in a deserted building. They both

had ideas of what to do with all the half empty rooms. The bedroom was fully furnished however, complete with bottles and jars on the dressing table glinting in the half dark with curtains drawn.

"Who lives here?"

He closed the door quickly. "It's a guest room. Sometimes I have friends over to play cards all night. This other room has a brick bed, I was going to have it taken out and put in floor boards so we can dance."

They made the round.

"Does the Third Miss Chu come here often?"

"Yes, she was here once or twice."

She did not talk much afterwards. Back in the parlor he said, "You're different. We'll always be together."

"Can't."

"Why?"

"Your wife."

"That was only on account of the Old Marshal. I've always been fair to her. After all it wasn't her idea. I'll come to some arrangement with her, but it's a matter between me and the Old Marshal." He always said the Old Marshal as if he was just one of his father's officers. Filial obedience was an old virtue that embarrassed him a little, he liked to put it under military discipline.

"No use saying anything just now, you're too young. It will only get you locked up."

"You said you'd come for me with a gun."

"Still best not to train a gun on a father-in-law."

She twisted away laughing. Somehow the new prospects did not surprise her. Their hopelessness had been no pretext with her, yet was already forgotten. Anything was possible after the miraculous coincidence of his loving her too.

"I wanted to give up this place but it's difficult to find another so near the house but out of the way. And there has to be room for the guards."

"What if they go and fetch me at the Marshal's House?"

"They'll telephone me. Plenty of time to get over there."

"Itchy." She pinned down the hands groping up her funnel sleeves.

"What's all this you've got on? It's too late today, I'll drive you to West Hill some time."

"You can drive?"

"It's easy."

"We can ride donkeys in West Hill."

"We'll rent donkeys. I'd like to live there. The foreign reporter Ronald has a villa there, did over a temple in the emperor's hunting park. He was telling about it the other day. In the first Chih-Feng war he walked around the front lines in West Hill and saw a wire trailing on the ground, so he picked it up and rolled it up as he went. Some of our men came yelling to him. He just stuck up a thumb and said, "Old Marshal very good," then shook his head: "Wu Pan-hu no good." They laughed and let him go. With the field telephone cut off the Manchurian army fell back and that turned the tide. So according to him he lost us the war."

"He wasn't afraid to tell it?"

"He invited me to come and see his electric bell wired with our piece of wiring. These foreigners think they're so brave. They walk into a rain of bullets and it stops, for fear of killing a foreigner. Where else but in China can you have such adventures without the least danger?"

"They say you like foreigners."

"They're fun to be with. More outspoken. I hate flatterers most of all." He leaned forward to knock off cigarette ashes and turned around to kiss her, a deer taking a lackadaisical sip from a pool. A lock of hair hanging down his brow, the head came down at her like a lowering sky or the quick nightfall in the mountains. She dipped dizzily into darkness.

It was still sunny afternoon and dead quiet with all the empty courtyards around them. Precisely because she was unused to such privacy her family seemed to be watching. Not her father whose remoteness and dignity made it inconceivable under the circumstances, but the others, the women of the house always waiting to put in a bad word, and Aunt Hung and her own amah who were responsible for her. They took the shape of birds carved roughly of unpainted wood perched on the rafters and over the door. She never looked up but she had some idea of them, round-eyed hook-beaked hens over a foot high, some larger, some smaller. She herself was up there looking down out of the wooden eye of double circles. His hand strained at her trouser leg and long silk under-pants and slid absently down the stocking. Sitting in his lap she had the oddest sensation of being flogged gently by some muffled piston or an atavistic thumping tail. The amahs had jokes about the tail bone at the base of the spine and had made her feel her own when she was a child. "It's the stump of the tail that has been cut off. Mankind had tails before." She doubted it happened even while it seemed to be going on underground. She did not want to ask him, it probably had to do with sex. Perhaps the only ladylike thing to do was to ignore it.

Starting from twilight the Drum Tower sounded every half hour with eight drum beats. The Bell Tower immediately tolled its answer, announcing the coming of night and the moral curfew.

"Funny I never noticed it before," she said. "It sounds like ancient times."

"The towers were built in Ming Dynasty."

"It's been like this every night since then?"

"Yes, the Manchus continued it."

"Why do we still do it? There're clocks now."

"Why indeed? We've been fifteen years a republic and nothing is changed."

He pulled a bell cord and shouted "Serve dinner" at the approach of footsteps. The dinner was set out in the next room with no one around. He smiled at her over his rice bowl. Eating at the same table by themselves they were real householders at last. Her embarrassments tied her in such knots she could not finish eating.

"What's the matter?"

"Nothing. You eat."

A new towel sprinkled with cologne was spread over a basin of hot water on the side table to keep it hot. When he had finished she put the towel in and wrung it dry for him, turning to go even before she had handed it over, ashamed of acting so wifely. Leaning away she smiled over her shoulder all in one quick movement. Entranced he caught her hand but she pulled away.

"Come out here," he called.

They looked at the moon on the corridor walk. He held her to him and the warmth of his loins swayed her back like a blown flame so that she laughed in surprise. The moonlight was blue on the scarlet pillars.

"Just think, I almost didn't come back."

She clutched him. "When? The last time you were in Mukden?"

"Yes, there was trouble. One of our officers turned on us. The Christian General was in it too."

"I seemed to have heard there was fighting outside the Pass."

"A near thing. The bulk of our troops marching on Mukden, only a few miles away. The Old Marshal's train all stoked up ready to leave."

"Leave for where?"

"Dairen."

"Dairen...That's where you were going."

"I suppose. I was cut off from Mukden at the time. There was even talk that I was mixed up in the uprising."

"How was that?" she whispered.

"Just because Koo and I belonged to the same company and got along all right."

"How can they say such a thing? Your own father. The Old Marshal didn't believe it?"

"The Old Marshal was very angry."

"But...Not now?"

"It's not mentioned any more. I was at fault of course, should have been more watchful."

That was more reason why he could not speak to his father about her or anything else just now. But all this was nothing compared to the chilling terror of their nearly missing each other, that seemed to dissolve his solidity right in front of her eyes and between her fingers. But here was the blue-limned face smiling down at her and the cool pressure of his lips. Here he was in Peking, the drum and bell continuing the night watch, louder outdoors, with a more pressing sense of the wonders and dangers of the night. For a moment it opened up the palaces and rabbit warrens of time behind the old city, all the double doors looking straight through one another as they swung open, to make a cavern or tunnel.

"You'd better go," he said. "We won't go by the same car."

"Fifth Old Concubine is so fond of you," Aunt Hung said. "Why not adopt you?"

"I don't want it."

"Silly. It's good to have a rich adopted mother. She'll make a good match for you."

"Aunt Hung never says a decent thing." She slumped forward to rest her chin on the table, fiddling with little objects at hand.

"No, really. Leave it to your father and you'd be given away as present. Of course this is just between you and me."

"Talk away, nobody's listening."

"I know you won't tell."

Was there a double meaning? No. She quickly put it out of her mind.

"Your Aunt Hung didn't say anything?" he asked.

"No."

"If they know you come here where we're all by ourselves

they'd certainly think you've been taken advantage of. Have you?" Laughing he tried to look into her face which she kept turned away. "Have you?"

She clung to the side of the sofa bending over it.

"If they really ask you what are you going to say?"

"The truth."

"Then it's still not too late for them to marry you off."

"Then I'll lie," she said after a moment.

"That's no use. Well, worst come to the worst I'll kidnap you."

"The Old Marshal will be very angry."

"That goes without saying. He has a special regard for your father."

"What shall we do?"

"Nevermind. I'm in bad standing with the Old Marshal anyway."

She did not like to lie down beside him on the sofa but this way they were able to gaze into each other's face longer than ever. The only annoying thing was that each had one arm too many. After various efforts to tuck it away he said, "Chop it off." The afternoon sunlight made a small rainbow on the wall mirror. She could not remember ever having known such peace and safety. Not a thought stirred in the golden desert-like calm with the mountain ridge of the sofa back looming on the horizon. It began to get dark in the room. Her smile deepened with the twilight. A look of dread pinched his eyes small. He buried his face in her loosened hair, wavy from the braiding.

"I don't know why, just now you were like a ghost."

"What kind of ghost?"

"The usual. A man lost his way and came upon a big house in the wilderness. He was invited in for dinner with the beautiful lady of the house. After spending the night together he walked out and looked back and no house, just a burial mound where the house had stood."

So he was afraid like her that it was all make-believe inside this door.

"There's that feeling of no night or day, just a dim yellow-brown sun like in the city of the dead."

"It's because we're cooped up here all day."

"I've never spent so much time with anybody in all my life," he laughed embarrassedly. "People are asking what I'm so busy at these days, why I'm never around."

"I wonder what they are saying behind your back."

"I'm dying to tell them."

"I won't mind if they say I'm your slave girl."

Slave girl was easier to say than concubine. But even as she was saying it, feeling moved by it herself, there was a faint suspicion at the back of her mind. Perhaps she was capable of shouting any time *"Pieng ni duh,* fooled you!" and run out laughing. She could stop any time. She would sit in his lap, the unbuttoned flap of her jacket hypocritically kept in place, the layers of opened trousers top and untied belts piled around her middle. There was something terrifying about the long reach down those warm folds and her hiding in the cupboard waiting to be discovered. His touch palpitated like a heart pumping thunders of blood through her and a listening silence. Their faces were close, yet remote, both with eyes down, idols towering half out of the little temple they shared, contemplating the thief in the dark prying at the ruby eye in the navel.

His head rubbing furrily against her bare breast frightened and revolted her slightly. Where did she get such a grown son to suckle? She saw him first regarding the goosepimply pink nipple with an expressionless eye before taking it in his mouth. The half itchy drawing on it also grated and needled like pressing it through a wire sieve. She looked down worriedly at the small pale triangle being flattened as he turned to the other one. Finally he raised his head blindly, a red haze over the eyes, and picked up his cigarette. She straightened her clothes and went to the mirror to tidy her bangs. Shaded by the big black square, now in place, she smiled at him and covered the slight awkwardness by stretching her arms downward with fingers interlaced in the attitude of a suppressed yawn. This jerked her sleeves up like the uptilted roof corners of a pavilion, and under the trousers the white L's of feet, stockings and slippers all white. He extended a hand without lifting it and she flew back to his side.

Being ignorant of any kind of basic rule between the sexes, even lying naked under him she felt free to get up and leave any time. A soft weightless bag made a disconcerting vacuum in the middle of her load. She ran her hand up and down his narrow back but when he grew restive she was close-faced and rigid. This had to wait for the "cave room and flowered candles", the wedding night going back to the cave-dweller's time. Even he would blame her if she did not keep something back for that night. And although she would not let herself think it, what if this house was to turn into a burial mound behind her one day the minute she stepped out the door? What happened here was only between the two of them, melting away without a trace when they each went back to their lives outside.

He remembered an appointment he could not get out of. The car would come back for her. She realized afterwards that he was a little angry, which was enough to make her feel lost.

"This is the only way. Then nobody can do anything about us ever," he said.

She nodded slightly with her head turned away on the sofa cushion. They never went near the bedroom.

"No, it's impossible," she said half laughing as if asked to swallow a bottle or rather a grooved ringed earthen jar.

"It hurts."

"It won't in a minute." He stopped several times.

"No, it hurts."

"We have to get this settled today."

The senseless ramming went on, as impossible as ever, now getting to be a racking pull splitting her into two. A sudden rush of air was forced up her chest. Between tossings of her head from side to side she saw him look thoughtfully into her face.

"I feel like throwing up."

He kept kissing her and hurrying back to his business, traditionally called the joy of fish in water and the dance of mandarin ducks with necks crossed. More like a dog butting at a tree stump for some reason of its own. She burst out laughing, finally laughing so hard there were tears in her eyes. He grinned ruefully, deflated. After a final crouch on all fours to examine the ground closely he stretched out to kiss her lightly and hold her to his side.

"It counts as done," he said face-savingly.

Peace returned and with it the luxury of pretending they could fall asleep and stay the night. To her surprise he was asleep. The Chinese room with western furniture had changed curiously in the dark yellow light of the standing lamp. The familiar tables and bureaus were ranged lower all round, farther away, backed against the wall to keep out of the fight. He lay curled up on his side, suddenly common-looking and unknown, the first man newly created that could be anybody, not worth the labors that produced him.

But it always seemed years before they met again and left her quite changed. They grinned at each other with the secret between them. It made them sit apart and talk of other things. When he pulled her to her feet she said no, it would hurt.

"We have to fix this."

He pulled her by the hand toward the sofa. There seemed a long way to go and the length of their arms left her a few steps behind. She found herself walking in a procession of muffled women. His wife and the others? But they had no identity for her. She joined the line as if they were the human race.

5

"The sound of the wind is not good these few days," Aunt Hung and the amahs were whispering.

She thought the fighting was over in Manchuria? Something about an assassination just outside Peking. Nobody went out. The front gate was barred with big water jars pushed against it. If the Young Marshal's car had come for her she was not even told.

She had already gone to bed when her amah came in and whispered straight-faced, "The Young Marshal is here."

He was at the door. She dressed hurriedly.

"Surprised?"

"So late!" she said, as if otherwise there was nothing

untoward about receiving men guests in the bedroom. The amah was gone, appropriately leaving the door slightly open.

"How did you get in?"

"I forced my way in. I told you I would if you don't come."

"You didn't."

But he was in uniform complete with pistol in holster.

"Does the front of the house know?"

"No, I came by the backdoor nearest you. A servant let me in. He knows who I am."

She thrilled at the magic of power that enabled him to pass through walls. It felt odd seeing him in this room that was outgrown, almost dingy, filled with the debris of childhood now behind her. But she was glad to break the spell that confined them to their phantom house. Here they were out in the everyday world. She had thought of him so much in this room. Couldn't he tell that? She used to come back at night when she had scarcely seen him at one of those birthday parties but with impressions so strong and so at odds with her old room she had to fix her eyes on the window as if listening to music. The reflection of weak lamplight browned the empty black panes framed in black-and-gilt wood. Without going to the window she was standing right in front of it, open to a damp wind blowing like a scarf on her face as the feeling came over her with the air of reality against her cheeks, then coming unstuck again, the multitude of filmy patterns drawing away, the exultant singing receding. Compared to such clamorous streams of sensations his actual presence here was ghostlike.

"Is there going to be fighting?"

"Lots of rumors around just now."

There was no telling whether the amah would help keep up the pretense by bringing tea. Perhaps she was starting the stove this minute.

"Everybody is staying home with locked doors?"

"Afraid of looting."

"Who are they afraid of? The Christian General has run away."

"There still are Fung's troops here. At the west city gate."

It was never quite clear to her how the Christian General kept on as a lesser partner to the Old Marshal, and still more confusing after their falling out.

"Who was this man that was assassinated?"

"Hsu Chow-ting," he mumbled looking away. Another of those names she was not supposed to remember. "It was Fung's doing."

"On a train."

"Yes. I could have been on that train." He half laughed.

"What?" That other world of his, the sea of unmemorable names and boring political dinners, suddenly reared up and flooded the room.

"I was at the dinner that saw Hsu off and he asked me to come along for the ride. I was thinking of running over to Tientsin anyway. They were going to mine the tracks, but with so many troop trains, the schedule was all upset. In the end they just dragged him off the train. That's how everybody knows who did it."

"How lucky you didn't go."

"That's why I was thinking, I don't care, I wanted to see you so I came."

She smiled back weakly. Was the amah coming back or no?

"Is the Old Marshal angry?"

"Of course. To have this happen so near the capital."

"Is there going to be war?"

"There's a lot of confusion just now. Premier Tuan has resigned. Hsu was his man. Just back from a trip abroad."

He got up and closed the door.

"No, you better go."

"It's just as bad to go now as later."

She watched him hang his belt on the bed rails, the dreamlike juxtaposition of the pistol holster against the bulbous iron railings ringed with faded gold.

"Aunt Hung is sure to hear."

"She probably knows already."

"No she doesn't."

"Everybody has gone to bed."

"She can see my light is still on."

"Turn it off."

"No, don't. I want to see you or I wouldn't know who it is."

He looked displeased at the very idea that there could be anybody else. But she had to see his face hanging over her like a lotus risen out of the sea, otherwise she wouldn't know what was happening to her, just pain in the darkness. The mosquito net was half tucked up so he could grab the pistol in case of emergency. If this got known what was to happen to Aunt Hung? And the amah? She was fouling their lots, making it impossible for them to go on with their meagre lives in this house. It was sinful, yet curiously safe like burrowing into the attic. For once they had the whole night, as lifelong as to the insects cheeping in the courtyard. She liked the first contact when she seemed to be getting him at last, a soft smooth flesh bait coolly slipping out of the toothless bites, a tantalization that melted the knees. But it became painful immediately.

"Say something nice to me so I can finish right away. Say you're Chan Shu-tan's man."

Somehow she just could not say it.

"Say you like me."

"I like you. I like you."

Off he went on his frantic ride and rode on after an arrow shot in the back made him grunt and pant, finally falling forward still hanging on, the hot flood pouring out of him.

"There're mosquitoes."

"Were you bitten? Where?" He licked a fingertip and rubbed the spot.

She smiled. He must have learned that as a small boy in the country. They were still safely in the middle of the night. He was a toy she could take to bed with her, a jade piece to fondle beside the pillow. With the light out she could just make out his profile facing up.

"You're not as happy as I am." She thought he looked sad.

"It's because I'm older. Like a child that cried and cried for an apple, still sniveling when he has got it."

"You've always had everything you wanted."

"No, I didn't."

She was sorry and wished she could go into all the years without her, the deserted courtyards yellowed by an ancient sun. She would rush in shouting "I'm here! I'm here!"

He leaned over the side to light a cigarette from the incense coil on the floor, supposed to keep mosquitoes away.

"All the talk was about Hsu Chow-ting at tonight's dinner."

"Why was he killed anyway?"

"He was getting up a coalition against the Christian General. The southeast gave him a royal welcome on his way back. But he was made much of everywhere. He was asked to review troops in England. When he found there were only two seats on the platform for the king and queen he looked displeased. So George V got up and let him sit with Queen Mary while he stood with the officers."

"Was he an army man?"

"Foreigners called him General Hsu. They call everybody general. He's a politician really. Little fat man. At a garden party in Buckingham Palace his senior secretary brought his wife, over fifty, with bound feet and dressed in Chinese clothes, but her husband wanted her to wear a big straw hat with flowers. A young secretary was against it. But her husband being a scholar with an imperial degree, second grade, knew everything in the world. 'Is there a foreign woman who'd go out in daytime without a hat?' he said. It was about six hundred yards to the royal tent and her bound feet could not walk fast. The wind blew her hat off. The young officer ran to get it but it rolled left and right and up and down and took a long time to catch. George V laughed with both hands holding his belly."

She tried not to be heard laughing from outside the room. He pulled her hand over and closed it around the sleeping bird, strangely tame and small, wrinkled and a little moist.

"Hsu spoke to the young man afterwards: 'You may not have stopped to consider, it's great disrespect to the English king.' The secretary said, 'Then what about the American chief justice? He was slapping the king's back, jumping up and down laughing.' Hsu said no more. The next day the London Times gave an account of the chase without comment, but criticized Chief Justice Hughes although he's an old friend of the king."

"Where else did they go?"

"America. All over. In Russia Hsu had a debate with their foreign minister Chinchirin. There he was welcomed as a head of state."

"Why?"

"No Chinese is taken seriously unless he's a military man. And he was an old-timer of the Pei-yang clique."

"I'd like to see Paris and Italy."

"We'll go. In a couple of years."

The drum and bell towers sounded the half hour. They were still deep inside China, deeper and older by the minute as the warning against dangers in the dark led far back into the centuries.

"Old Tuan telegraphed him at Shanghai not to come back. Old Tuan was afraid for him. But he thought it would be an international joke if the Special Envoy dared not come back to Peking. Also because of the fighting in Manchuria, he thought to take advantage of the situation, the old fox. He saw a chance for Old Tuan. So he borrowed a car from the British consulate in Tientsin and was driven to Peking flying the British flag on the radiator cap. Somehow he didn't take precautions this time. It's fate."

"He just took a train."

"Yes, supposed to be a special train, just a car hitched to the regular train. Brass bands to welcome him at every stop and a long wait to water the engine. The station was brightly lighted and surrounded with troops, as grand as his reception in Moscow. An officer came aboard and asked for Mr. Hsu. The Envoy is not feeling well, his secretary said and asked the man to sit in the upper seat but he took the lower."

"Even on a train there's an upper and lower seat?"

"Not berths either. With us Chinese it's always ceremony first, war later. So they chatted. The officer said he was sent by Commander Chang and where was Mr. Hsu? The secretary insisted he was not well. Hsu was in another compartment sleeping off his wine. The voices woke him up. He came out rubbing his eyes. 'Didn't I tell you the Envoy is not well?' the secretary said."

He pulled her hand back.

"The officer stood up. When Hsu finally got them all seated again he said, 'I'm not feeling well, had to refuse all invitations along the way.' 'Commander Chang has been waiting all evening. Will Mr. Hsu please alight.' 'There's no time.' 'The train will wait.' 'I have vicious influenza. I'll call on the Commander another time.' 'There's a tea party at headquarters to welcome Mr. Hsu.' 'What tea party, at midnight?' 'Urgent consultation.' 'What's so urgent? I've already sent somebody to Mongolia to talk over everything with Mr. Fung.' And the secretary put in, 'Mr. Fung and Mr. Hsu are like one family. Nothing between them that cannot be arranged.' But the officer signalled with a handkerchief and about a dozen soldiers swarmed up and helped Hsu off the train."

"How is it they still have headquarters near here?"

"They're winding up their affairs along the railroad."

She would never understand how two war lords could share Peking each with a railway to himself, and one allowing the other to clear out in such a leisurely fashion after a fight.

"They shot him at headquarters?"

"No, no, in the fields, pitch dark. A great scandal as it is. The Christian General stamping his feet at the way they bungled his plan."

These people became little funereal dolls in green glaze jackets and yellow pants with worn earthen patches, that they could examine together with their heads on one pillow mat.

"Old Tuan himself touched it off. He'd always played Fung off against us, now he was scared at the upset, worried what Fung was going to do next, cornered in Mongolia, his hundreds of thousands of troops falling apart. So this is what he did next. The news of Old Tuan not coming to office for several days so unnerved him he struck down the old man's righthand man. Left to himself Old Tuan is terrified of him, dared not talk loud even in his own house."

"He'd hear in Mongolia?"

"He has spies everywhere. Everybody is followed. He'd know I'm here tonight."

She was electrified and almost had a warm feeling for the Christian General, the confidante who would not tell on them.

"Wouldn't it be dangerous when you go out of here?"

"No."

"There's not going to be war?"

"I guess there still has to be a show-down."

"Because of the assassination?"

"Well anyway, with Hsu dead his anti-Communist coalition seems to be coming true. Everybody set on toppling Fung."

"He's a Christian and a Communist too."

"He's a fake. Russia pays him sixty thousand a month not counting all the arms he get."

"Then he's not a real Communist, just pretending?"

"That doesn't make him any better. To hear people talk of the red menace, it's *hung shui mung sheuh*, great flood and predatory animals. It seems to me there are worse things, in a country where everybody's so poor. I suppose to older people it means the end of all standards. Like the Old Marshal, Communists are the one thing he hates."

"There aren't many?"

"We've caught many. Some college students too. A pity they were used by Russia."

"They're killed when they're caught."

"Yes."

She had seen the occasional head strung on the electric pole by the city gate. "Don't look," the amah would say as their car or ricksha passed it. She just got an impression of all the features on the face being pulled up by the roots of the hair like Peking opera actors who wear these tight net kerchieves. A red streak here and there on the cheek and over the brows seemed part of the make-up. She was afraid but as long as nobody knew who it was—The wash amah Li Paw had once said that a man from her village was caught. She told the story when they were all sitting in the courtyard taking the breeze at night, the amahs on low stools, Fourth Miss lying on her back on a cot of sliced bamboo that made a smooth slab as cold as a tombstone. The big black sky pin-pointed with stars bore down on her with all its weight, a tremendous crushing dome that the eye could not endure. She was looking for the Dipper lying down as in an old poem. That summer night itself seemed like a thousand years ago, although it had been right outside here in the same courtyard.

"Selling candy dolls when they caught him and took him to Headquarters. Catching people all over."

"That's the way it is nowadays," said another amah. Everybody spoke in a scratchy whisper when it came to current affairs.

"Scares you to death to hear them tell it. On the day of execution the judge sits behind the aproned table, with two lines of soldiers before him carrying rifles. The four prisoners kneel in a row. Four markers are lying on the table, stuck on bamboo splits. The judge checks the names, picks up his writing brush and runs a red stroke through the name on a marker and tosses it down like a spear. At this all the guards give a big yell. One of them snatches it up and sticks it on the back of a prisoner's collar. One by one all four are marked. Suddenly the judge kicks the table over, turns and runs away. To scare off the *shah*."

"What's that?" said Fourth Miss. The others tittered at her question.

"Never heard of the return of the *shah*?" Aunt Hung said. "The dead coming back three days after death."

"*Shah* is the ghost?"

"Or the demon of death itself. I don't really know. Ask Li Paw."

"They say it's a big bird. People hide on the day the *shah* returns, to keep out of harm's way. But some were curious and sprinkled ashes on the floor. They found bird prints."

"*Shah* is said to be around whenever there is killing or even a thought of killing," Aunt Hung said. "That's why the judge has to protect himself."

She was sitting up by now glad to be surrounded by familiar figures in the dark.

"The prisoners stripped to the waist are paraded on a mule cart, a column of troops in front, a column behind and two rows on either side. The execution supervisor comes at the end riding a horse, with a red sash over his shoulder like a bridegroom. Two trumpeters clear the road blowing the foreign tune for the charge, da da dee da da dee. And all the soldiers yell, '*Sha*-ah! Kill!' And the crowd shouts after them, '*Sha*-ah!'"

"Tch! These people," said another amah.

Another half snickered. "At the gate house they always say

'Go see the beheading.' "

"These men! And with so much time to themselves. Not like us."

"Go on, Li Paw, what happens next?" said Fourth Miss, and this also made them laugh.

"What happens? Outside the city gate the four are lined up kneeling. The executioner comes up to the first man, claps him hard on the back of the neck for size, swings the sword once and kicks the head away. He was getting to number four who saw it all. That was the man from my village. He fainted, and woke up lying on the prison floor. He was the execution companion."

"Execution companion," Aunt Hung bit into the words dubiously. "Yes, there's the guest of honor and there're others invited just to keep him company."

"They let him out in a couple of days. They weren't so sure he was a spy."

"Then why didn't they just keep him in prison?" Fourth Miss said.

"And feed him for years? They just wanted to give him a scare. But he died a few months after he got home."

"Fear split his gall and no wonder," Aunt Hung said.

"Hey ya, in times like these," said Li Paw, "It's a good thing that in a big deep house you don't get to hear things."

Somehow she did not feel like telling him the story although it was before his time. It must have been in Wu Pan-hu's days. Surely they did things differently now? But he was always touchy on the point that nothing really changed.

He flicked cigarette ashes into the incense dish on the floor. "I've got a sore throat from whispering."

"Don't let's talk."

"We'll fall asleep."

"Maybe you'd better go now. Before it's light."

He reflected for a moment. "It's all right. I'll wake up before five."

"How do you know you would?"

"I'm used to it in camp."

"If there is war you'll be going." She had tried not to say this.

"I'll have somebody watch out for you."

"Do you ever sleep with your hand here?"

"When I was little. It seemed the safest place to put it, somehow."

"Me too, but the amah always pulled it away so I stopped doing it."

But his hand tucked between her legs seemed all right, like hand in pocket. He woke her with a kiss. It was grey all round.

"No. No, aren't you going?" She cried when he threw a leg over her and slid up.

For a while it was not sore. She was still half dreaming cradled on a rough sea. Their boat had gone out in the eerie uniform greyness. But their stale faces smelled safe, reminder of a night's sleep in bed.

She sat up as he dressed, snatching a feel at his shoulders, back and elbows.

"Don't get up. The man will be around to show me out."

"Don't wear your shoes."

He hesitated a moment. It would embarrass him. "No, it's all right."

She heard his footsteps going down the stone-paved corridor, excruciatingly distinct to the end. Her heart went cold. She knew for certain now that Aunt Hung knew. Still she tidied the bed and picked up the cigarette butts in the tin dish of incense coil. When she washed her face she managed to wash the hidden towel. Soaked in the basin of hot water it smelled faintly of thin rice gruel, also thought of as a source of life.

6

"Things are in great disorder outside," Aunt Hung confided. "Your father went and got up a local security council, same as when the dynasty fell. But what a change of position. The Old Marshal was just one of his officers then. This time he must have given permission or your father wouldn't have gone ahead with it."

Fourth Miss knew what was coming.

"Their eldest is a good boy, considering. He stood pampering well. Although his wife is no match for him, for all the talk about the Third Chu he never did take her into the house. That's something."

Fourth Miss did not flinch at this about the Third Chu. She

went on playing with the brass-ring puzzle.

"Actually in a family like theirs, what if there are two wives both just as great? The Old Marshal may not allow it for such a young man, but it may also have to do with the Chus' reputation. If it's a different kind of girl now, from a different sort of family. A girl's reputation is most important. People talk all over town before there is anything to speak of. Take your father, especially now that he's active again. Even if everybody knows of his connection with the Chans he wants at least to seem independent. What if people say he'd do anything to please the Chans? You know your father's temper. Even the Old Marshal won't interfere—after all a man punishing his own children. Not to say me, I'd be held guilty myself. I needn't go into all this, it must have occurred to you."

She herself was ready to die for it but what about Aunt Hung and her amah? They were her hell. Only she was not obsessed with hell. For the moment she was not expected to say anything as long as she bowed her head. Aunt Hung was being extraordinarily mild about it. Even then she could not help hardening and shrinking at the desecration of the thing between him and her merely by mentioning it. Just for other eyes to look on it was to misunderstand.

Aunt Hung said no more. The most important thing at the moment was to stop him from paying them another visit. He did not come again.

It was a point of honor with Fourth Miss not to ask him about the future. Just because he did not mention it did not mean he had forgotten. If he had tried speaking to his father and met with humiliations he would not want to tell her. He had never told her that he knelt for a whole day asking his father's forgiveness after the Manchurian rebellion. She heard this at a relatives' house.

She was never worried the minute she saw him. Everything was as clear as smiling into a mirror. Only when he had gone to war and she had not seen him for months her position began to weigh on her. She wanted to go to his house and see the Fifth Old Concubine and his children, even his wife. They were her only kin. At home she lived among strangers. The Fifth Old Concubine often spoke of him as a child:

"He used to wait by a pond in the courtyard for people in new clothes who seemed well-pleased with themselves. He'd throw a big stone into the water splashing all over them and clap his hands and laugh. People were too embarrassed to say anything except 'Did the Young Marshal get a fright?' Hey-ya, the naughtiness, and when he got older, the worries and jitters I had, from having to account for him before his father," she said proudly with her puffy eyelids down.

She owed her position largely to him. She had been a small town prostitute once. If he got killed in the war Fourth Miss saw herself go up to her and kneel down crying hugging her knees begging to be taken in. "Alive I am a person in his house; dead I shall be a ghost in his house" was the set piece on such occasions. The maiden went to her lover's funeral dressed in mourning:

"White silk blouse, white silk skirt,

White silk kerchief on black hair girt."

It would be a case of *wong mung gua*, widowed by looking at the door, when a girl who had lost her fiancé wished to be his widow. What was one more extra woman in that huge house already full of rickety relationships, an old concubine he treated as his mother, an oldish woman he treated as his wife. They wouldn't refuse her? She was too young to know her own mind and would ruin their good name by remarrying eventually. The usual reason. She would be forcibly escorted back to her own house where her father would kill her from shame.

He telephoned just before the Lunar New Year. "It's me.

I'm back."

At the sound of his voice she seemed suddenly to lean back against solid wall although she had not moved from where she stood telephone in hand. The car was coming for her.

"Back?" Aunt Hung said.

"Yes."

The trouble Aunt Hung had had in getting a telephone of her own, the suspicions it aroused were justified now that a tryst had been arranged over it. She had a guilty pang at Aunt Hung's silence. As for the amah, the woman stole around nowadays as if pregnant by a ghost, expecting to give birth to some monster any day now.

He had won the battle of the South Pass after a long siege. He got dysentery at the front. Opium was recommended as a quick cure so he got the habit.

"I'll have a doctor end it as soon as I'm rested."

He would not let her see him lie down and smoke, wrapping his lips around the thick mouthpiece to make a slightly tilted snout. It was the vice of his father's generation like singsong girls. Both smelled of old men's spit.

"Did you miss me?" With an arm around her he strained to see her averted face. The question was sexual somehow. "Did you miss me?"

She finally gave a half-hearted stiff-necked nod.

"Do you smell it on my breath?"

"No." It was just a faint odor you associate with old people. She thought of opium as a handicap of the elderly. Still it was fortunate this was all he got from the war.

"The Third Chu is going to be married."

"Really? To whom?"

He muttered a name.

"What does he do?"

"Politician. She could have done better."

They spoke of other things. She suddenly smiled widely at him and burst out with, "I'm so glad."

"I knew you were dying to say that." He half laughed irritably and seemed to resent the comforting arms she put around him.

The next day he telephoned after eight in the evening. "It's me. I want to see you once more this year."

It immediately seemed to her also that it would be a year's separation otherwise. "Too late today."

"Tomorrow is New Year's Eve."

"No, that won't do."

"Say it's a show. The car comes right now."

"All right."

"I'm to go to the show with them," she mumbled to Aunt Hung.

"Tch! With the New Year upon us every family has business of its own. Nobody goes gallivanting around. Your father will speak," she whispered and it sounded frightening, his speaking at all.

After a silence Aunt Hung turned to the amah murmuring, talking fast, "Go up front and say the Marshal's House is taking Fourth Miss to a show."

The amah went.

"Well, hurry up and get ready, in case nothing is said. You can't go out like this."

They really went to see a movie. This started him taking her to shows and dinners where there was dancing. Either he was growing reckless or wanted to force the issue. His doctor always went along to give him injections for the opium cure. She had her hair done up to look as if it was cut, and wore new gowns and high heels kept at their secret house. Everybody was talking about them but she did not mind, not like with Aunt Hung. This was just the crowd's murmur, part of the lights and music.

She did not get to hear what the Old Marshal said:

"Who can't he have for a concubine, it has to be my old friend's daughter. What kind of man does that make me? Marriage is out of the question even if he's free. We Chans don't have daughters-in-law that are laid first and married later."

Her father made his first move.

"I spoke to the principal of Peking University," he summoned her to say. "He will let you in as a listening student. You can try to catch up in a year or two."

No reason was given why she alone of the brothers and sisters was to go to school. The assumption was times were changing, college girls were sometimes preferred in marriage. In effect it set her free with the entire school day at her own disposal. If she went to the bad the blame was on modern education, the usual whipping boy. Better let her run wild than have it said that her father gave her away as concubine to the Chans. It eased the unspoken strain between the two houses. If the affair came to nothing she might still marry. Didn't the Third Chu?

Aunt Hung was oddly triumphant, the first time Fourth Miss had ever seen her excited. All these years of neglect and slights were avenged. The man was afraid. Her child had backing that had him cowed. Fourth Miss was her daughter as never before. She allowed herself to worry aloud:

"The times are unsettled. Better make your plans, don't put it off too long. Of course the Old Marshal is in a difficult position because of his feeling for the Tangs. But you don't want to fight over an empty name. Out of regards for your father he can't treat you wrong. The thing is for the Young Marshal to find the right person to speak to his father, someone who could get a word in. It's up to you to make up your mind. Men are never in a hurry," she whispered smiling, leery of calling attention to her knowledge of men as a singsong girl, careful not to hint that he might be as fickle as others. "I'm just reminding you as a bystander. I can see you don't lack decision. People will blame me for not speaking up earlier. For one thing it would be no use. It will just spoil things after being mother and daughter together."

Fourth Miss remained silent. By now it was rude and hurting never to have told her anything. But how was she to tell her that they never spoke of such things?

"So the Third Chu is married. Even got her husband a post. That's modern times for you."

Aunt Hung seemed particularly impressed by her keeping

quiet about the Third Miss Chu's marriage. It made her slightly uneasy to have come to be loved for her supposed hardness.

Moon Festival was celebrated as usual in Peking despite the war with Canton, now split into Nanking and Hankow on their way north. He had been away for a long time on the Honan front. Still it was the happiest Moon Festival in her life. She had a schoolmate over, a girl alone in Peking, and walked her back to the dormitory. The family ricksha followed a few paces behind so they could ride any time they got tired. The low grey houses made the streets look still wider. Firecrackers pit-patted faraway with now and then a surprise banging away hollowly close by. All the shops were boarded up, everybody home by now for the reunion feast. The long street led straight up to the slate blue sky with the moon like a wheel of ice. The wind blew her veil into her mouth every time she spoke. She wore the dark red knitted shawl that no college girl was without and swung the box of moon cakes that her friend was to take home with her. They walked on the tram tracks until a tram bore down on them as big as a house clacking its bell that sounded like "I got the best man, the best, the best, the best." It was exactly what she had wanted when she stood right in front of the stage as a child with both hands on the boards and could never get up close enough. Now the cymbals were clapping down on top of her head.

He telephoned the next day. It turned out that he had come back the day before.

"Spent Moon Festival with his wife," Aunt Hung sniggered, indignant.

She just smiled. She herself had had to eat reunion feast with the family.

"Where's Dr. Liang?" she looked around the room when he made her sit down beside him.

"That turtle egg, I threw him out."

"What happened?" She had never seen him so angry.

"Those injections he gave me was a kind of morphine."

"Stop opium with morphine?"

"It's on purpose. To get me into the habit."

"Why, who is he?"

"He turns out to be Yang Yi-peng's man."

She searched her glossary of faceless names. Would that be the Old Marshal's most trusted aide?

"Why?"

"He hates me. It's all out in the open after the Koo Sing-ling incident."

The uprising in Manchuria. He didn't mean he was in it after all?

"That was to get him mainly."

Only partly against his father? The enormity of it instantly put her at sea. What happened to crown princes who rose against their father? Imprisonment, an imperial gift of poisoned wine for which you kowtowed in thanks toward the direction of the palace. Whatever he did it showed he was a man, not just So-and-so's son. Maybe she was also a little sad because he had done what he wouldn't do for her sake.

"But they say that you—" She stopped.

"That I lost my head gambling and whoring, didn't know what was going on in my own battalion?"

"Just that you were careless."

"I'm not such a fool. I played cards with Koo at the battalion club, yes. He's one of our better young officers. We both wanted change, but no chance of that as long as Yang was around. In the end there was no other way. It would have succeeded too but for the Japanese intervention."

"Why are they for the Old Marshal?"

"They don't want the Russians in Manchuria. Koo was allied with the Christian General and he's with the Russians."

She could not imagine him on the Christian General's side against his father. Since then he had defeated the General at South Pass. This year the two had been fighting again in Honan with the General on the side of the south.

Her silence made him add in his father's defence, "Some say the Old Marshal is pro-Japanese. Of course he has to get along with them because Manchuria is right next to Korea. But he always took this attitude: the small things could be talked over, the big things he would put off. Nowadays even the small things he will put off, the big things are definitely not negotiable. He never even carried out their terms for squashing Koo Sing-ling."

"What happened to Koo?"

"He was shot."

For a moment neither of them spoke. He had been spared because he was the son.

"Can't you tell the Old Marshal about being tricked? About the injections."

A slight shake of his head with a half blink dismissed the idea completely. But meanwhile other people would be telling the Old Marshal about his turning into an addict at his age.

"A funny thing the other day, shows the kind of people we

have around. Word came that the southern troops violated the first president's grave, so somebody suggested that we desecrate Sun Yatsun's body in return."

"Sun Yatsun is buried here?"

"In West Hill. Luckily Yieh Loh-fu was around that day, an old Nationalist. He persuaded the Old Marshal that these things were not done nowadays and anyway to check first. It turned out to be not the Nationalists but the Christian General's garrisons. Trees were chopped down, buildings robbed but the grave was untouched. So Yieh said to the Old Marshal, since Sun's remains happen to be in Peking we should protect it just to show we are big-hearted. So the Old Marshal ordered a detail of soldiers to the Temple of Green Clouds. Sure enough, in a couple of days several men went to the temple with picks and hoes. When they saw the sentries they loitered and left."

"Who were they?"

"Chi Yung-fu's men."

She gathered that they were from the first president's old troops.

"We're not so far behind. Why, the Nationalists themselves, two years ago when their rightists lost power to the left they came all the way here from Canton, into enemy territory as it was, just to hold a meeting in front of their leader's grave, and was known henceforth as the West Hill Conference Clique. Madame Sun herself—it was her idea to embalm him to last forever."

"He looks alive?" she cried.

"Yes, she got the idea from Lenin, she's pro-Communist. Of course she put it on her husband, said he had said it would be best if the body could be preserved. His followers were rather taken aback. For one thing the costs. In the end Russia gave them the glass coffin as a gift."

"Is she beautiful?"

"Big eyes."

"Which is more beautiful, she or her younger sister?"

"The younger is more lively. Madame Sun is lively too except that her husband took sick right away when they were here. I represented the Old Marshal to welcome him off the ship in Tientsin. It snowed the day we got to Peking. As we drove from the station there was a huge crowd besides the welcoming groups. People on top of all the roofs and trees with the big snow coming down." He confronted her almost indignantly. "The crowd was just as big in Tientsin, only the police chief drove them away to please Premier Tuan."

"Was Sun Yatsun really such a great man?"

"The thing is he represents the idea of a republic. At the revolution most people didn't know what happened. By the thirteenth year of the republic they really got to want it. Like women, when they are first married they don't know what it's all about but later they come to want it. Will you?"

"I don't know. I'm not married." She was sorry the minute it was out of her mouth, as if to remind him.

"So you're not. Getting independent, eh? Say whose man you are."

"Stop it."

"Whose man are you? Say it."

"Stop it. Was Madame Sun's sister with them that time?"

"No, just the two of them. He'd been invited down to form a government. There were high hopes among his followers that he'd be president. He called on the Old Marshal as soon as he arrived. I was with them. After the greetings the Old Marshal stood up right away saying, 'I Chan am a rough man, so I'd like to say frankly, it's my business to boost men. Today I may boost a man named Tuan. So can I boost a man named Sun. I only object to Communism. If we are to practise Communism I Chan would rather shed blood than go red.' This little speech when it got to Tuan's ears made him more suspicious than ever. Actually the talk only lasted half an hour. Sun of course denied he was pro-Communist. But there was Tuan, already installed. Sun went back to his hotel and conferred with his aides until after midnight. That same night he got ill."

"That's how he died!"

"A few months later. All this time Old Tuan wouldn't see him and never went to the funeral. The excuse was his legs were so swollen he could not get into his shoes. The head of a country and no shoes to wear!"

"At least he's gone away."

"He's having a good laugh on us. The government a vacuum after he stepped down. The regency cabinet with all our allies represented couldn't last of course. After the cabinet resigned nobody else would accept the posts. The Old Marshal was angry. 'Then just get anyone,' he said. Government employees have not been paid for six months. Ex-emperor Pu Yi still gets thirty thousand a month, from us personally. This respect for all higher-ups is all that's left of our king and country. Anyway all the people ever ask for is 'a Honan man to rule Honan' and 'a Shantung man to rule Shantung.' If they must be misruled they'd rather have one of themselves do it. As far as possible we let them have it. Any local person with enough armed men to overrun the area, gets from us a title or a post."

It did not sound good. "Is the war going to get here?"

"There's no telling about wars. As far as strength goes we have no fears. Last year Fung's troops did exceptionally good trench work at South Pass. But our cannons were so fierce, after several days of concentrated firing even the earth crust was turned over. Canton belonged to the school of revolutionaries with home-made bombs. Now that they have Russian arms and advisors naturally our allies are no match for them. Like Wu Pan-hu, when news came that his front was collapsing he sent the Big Sword Corps to chop down deserters. His soldiers had heard the Big Swords were coming and took shots at them through the train windows. The swordsmen never dared get off the train."

"What's the use of these allies?"

"Yes, everybody for himself. Fang of the southeast just sat still watching Wu get hit when he could have easily cut off the southern supply lines. When he was defeated in turn he bribed Long Legs to give him safe conduct to Mukden so he could come beg for help in person, traveling incognito in civilian clothes because he was a disgrace to the uniform. Seeing how he humbled himself the Old Marshal sent Long Legs to help him get back his five provinces." She had heard of their General Long Legs. "The Old Marshal is like that. As long as a man is your equal, even if he has been an enemy, always be generous and save him some face. The worst offence is to move against your superior. That's how Long Legs ganged with Fang managed to flatter the Old Marshal into heading the government himself. Subordinates don't count, but the support of your peers..."

"Has he become President?" she faltered.

"No, not President or Premier, just Grand Marshal. The Old Marshal is modest that way. All his life he has preferred to stay in the wings. This is already unlike him."

He stopped abruptly. She had also heard the saying, "Change and die." It was a bad sign when older people change their ways.

"The south is a mess too," she said.

"They have their kit of tools."

"They're Communists?"

"Not any more. Nanking has hitched a thread on England and America and thrown over Russia. Now Russia is looking to us to stop the south. The Old Marshal doesn't care, he had the Soviet Embassy searched anyway and published all the secret documents, proofs of their subversions. They're pushing hard here. It did look as though they had China going Communist."

"In the south?"

"Everywhere the southern troops went. Mass trials of landlords. Dividing up the land. Cutting men's gowns short, the long gown is upper class. Also attacking churches and missions like the Boxers all over again. Foreigners do get themselves hated because the government kowtows to them and takes their part, then as now. A missionary is a power in the countryside. It's always popular to be against foreigners, and Communism sneaks in under cover. The people have their grievances and will have it out any way you let them. But the Communists are being purged, they lasted no longer than the Boxers."

"Is Madame Sun's sister married now?"

He smiled. "I don't know, haven't heard."

"How old is she?"

"About my age."

"She's not twenty-seven already?"

"I don't know, she herself didn't say. Foreignized women don't tell their age."

"She can't be not marrying ever?"

"There's no telling about those Christians."

"It's not because of you?"

"No, no."

"She must have liked you."

"She was looking for a ruler of China and I stood a chance of inheriting the position."

"You make her sound so hard."

"It's only natural that she should want to emulate her sister."

"Is she very beautiful?"

"No."

"No, tell the truth."

"There is a wonderful freshness that comes with going to school abroad. And she didn't come back all masculine and insufferable."

"Lucky the Old Marshal wouldn't let you get a divorce."

"It never came to that."

"Didn't you want to marry her?"

"If I did it had to do with the whole picture. A man may also want to marry into a certain house, like a lighted doorway everybody turns to—something you don't happen to have. After that crowd to see Sun Yatsun in the snow, any relations I can have with a man like that I won't mind having."

"But you have to like the girl."

"That of course. I used to get those ideas, not like now, no more stray thoughts."

"Did the Old Marshal know?"

"He took it as a joke. His son marrying the daughter of a fife-and-drummer! That's what they call her father. He used to play a harmonium doing missionary work near Shanghai."

The famous debutante was now a cozy figure in her own past. "I wonder why she never married."

"It may be difficult for her too. At her age, even a couple of years back all the men she met would be married."

He pulled the bell rope. The new doctor was fetched from another courtyard to give him the same injection as the other doctor had been giving him.

He was still pent up. "Let's go to West Hill."

"So late. The city gate will be closed."

"It will open for us."

It was growing dark as they got into the car with the doctor. They could hear from afar the gong at the city gate working itself up to a long frantic tzong-tzong-tzong-tzong-tzong-tzong, sounding an enemy attack or fire or flood, the end of the world. The car got round the mule carts that had just managed to squeeze in. One of the guards jumped off the running board and ran ahead shouting. The gates swung open again and they drove through the tunnel in the iron-grey wall standing on black dust.

The long ride really seemed to get them away. But at West Hill Hotel they did not go into the dining room in case there was somebody they knew. They stood around the goldfish pond while Dr. Li went in to order soft drinks. She was wearing black glasses and a veil.

"You look like a war lord's concubine meeting a female impersonator in secret," he said.

It was not so romantic though. They ate dinner in their suite upstairs with the doctor. They spoke of places to see in the morning before going back, so it was settled that they would stay the night. She could say she was at a schoolmate's house but she wondered if she was going too far.

It was unnaturally silent in the country and the western-style hotel was dead quiet. Peking seemed a long way off with its vigilant drum and bell and city murmurs. Staying out all night, and in a hotel, she was so far out of bounds that she was no longer under the protection of the law. She felt ridiculously like a captive bride brought to a new village, finally under his power.

Oddly enough he also looked embarrassed taking off his clothes not looking at her, smiling slightly, his eyes very bright. To escape the feeling of strangeness she quickly went to bed and under cover and slipped into his arms as soon as he got in. But he turned back the blanket and took his time sorting her out in the lamplight.

"What are you doing?"

An animal was feeding on her. She saw his bent head enlarged by perspective between her reared thighs and felt his hair brushing against her with a frenzy of terror. The flicks of his kisses furled petal-like in and around the bud of her inner self, intolerably. The resignation of the fallen prey alternated in her with some unformed yearning to get away somehow or devour in turn, be packed full of him. She tried to get up several times. At last it was him again smiling down at her, a little flushed. She took him almost gasping with relief, catching sips of a half glass of wine rocking on board ship. He filled her slowly with deep plunges and suddenly swung sideways like a fish swishing its tail, watching her face half laughing. He stopped to look and fondle.

"Bigger, aren't they? Haven't they grown?"

But they hardly talked all night, for a change.

7

Her father called her into his study and spoke in his deepest voice with an official ring.

"The political situation is tense. The Old Marshal is sending the family back to Mukden. Leaving tonight. He has sent for you. Perhaps it's best in times like these—saves worries on both sides. Out of his friendship for me he is sure to treat you like a daughter. On your part however you have to learn to behave from now on. It's up to you yourself now. Tell your Aunt Hung to pack for you but there's no need to bring many things or people. Whatever you want can always be sent for later. Just dress warmly, it's cold outside the Pass. When the times are more settled you can come back and your Aunt Hung can also go and see you."

She had a wonderful trip. The Chans on their special train received her as a niece coming for a long visit. The Young Marshal's wife took her on as her special charge. She was to call her Big Sister from now on instead of Big Sister-in-law. Outside the Pass was China's Arctic. Sad princesses and palace beauties had been sent out there to marry the kings of the Huns. She was agreeably surprised by the heaving brown mountains and the grey sash of the Great Wall draped across them, buckled with twin square citadels. The scene never changed in the window, a picture screen being busily folded away, clackety-clack, clackety-clack, and still no end to it.

At the first stop next morning she looked out at a box car of soldiers halted on the next line. The soldiers were standing as if half out of the car. A peasant boy red-cheeked from the cold was eating his breakfast of fritter and bun. His thin face and neck came out of the padded uniform like the end of the fritter stick stuffed into the big sesame bun. They were talking and laughing a few feet away, yet soundless. She stared with a pleasant shiver around the heart, what she later thought was presentiment. The day after she got to Mukden the Old Marshal coming back the same way was assassinated by a mine.

It was dangerous for the Young Marshal to come back but he managed it on troop trains dressed as a common soldier, with forced marches between rides.

When he turned up in the midst of the confusion and funeral preparations it was as if he had dropped down from heaven. He cried when he heard his father's last words were, "Has Little Six come back?" He was the sixth son of the clan.

He knew she was here. The aide stationed behind to take her out of the Pass in case of emergency had telegraphed him at the front.

"Father thought of us when he had so many things on his mind," he said to her.

"They say the Japanese did it," she said.

"Probably." His eyes shone curiously in the shadow of the army cap which he kept on even at night to hide the shaved head, part of the disguise.

To her it was a fitting end to their story, his coming back after such hardships. And they lived happily ever after. There was some truth in this ending to fairy tales which generally deal with young people and early success. What you get at that impressionable age stays with you. It was the only time when anyone can build things larger than life and in its own way lasting as long. At seventeen she had achieved the impossible, all that she had ever wanted. If there is a certain smugness in all young wives in addition to the reputed serenity of Oriental women, she was still more so, being younger and happier than any that she knew of. An unshakable placidity entered her soul like a second spine. Nothing that really mattered could happen to her any more.

"First we heard the Old Marshal had left for Mukden," he told her, "it looked as if we were retreating. We were fooling with a Ouija tray, it was a quiet night, so we thought to ask about the war. It wrote on the sand, 'The Grand Marshal is going home.' I was laughing, 'What wonderful fortune-tellers we are. Who doesn't know the Grand Marshal is going home?' That same night we got the telegram."

The train was wrecked on the railway bridge at the Fort of the Imperial Aunt.

He evidently found comfort in the story. If the supernatural exists in any way then maybe his father was still near. He was beset on all sides by the mourners sent by friends and foes alike. The Christian General, the Nationalists, the Japanese, the "king of Shansi" all had representatives at the funeral to pressure him into agreements, alliances, recognitions. He closed the Pass to

General Long Legs and left him to be mopped up. He stopped the subsidies to Japanese personnel in Manchuria and sent for W. F. Ronald, known as the man to have with you in a pinch.

"They say they shot two people here," her old amah whispered to her.

"Where?"

"Over in the office building."

One was Yang, she heard later, the one who had got him into the morphine habit. In the evening he came in to change.

"Oh, get me the dollar in the trousers pocket."

He liked to play with the coin and had it gold-plated. He hefted it in his hand smiling.

"Last night I couldn't make up my mind about Yang and Ho so I tossed the dollar."

"No!" she said dismayed.

"People have been telling me they're unstable." The dread words "revolt" and "coup" were seldom said outright. "But you can't tell, people are jealous, and my differences with Yang are well-known. Now is not the time to remember grudges. So finally I said to myself, head for arrest, tails for execution. Three times to make sure."

"All tails?"

"All three times. I thought maybe this coin is lighter on one side. Try three more times, head for execution. And three times all head."

She shrank from the first president's round moustachioed face on the proffered coin. She did not believe in superstitions but she believed in him. He put it out of sight in his pocket quickly.

"I feel bad because of the Old Marshal."

"He'll understand now," she said.

"After a single interview with Yang, just back from studying from Japan, he had him start the munitions plant. That's how the Old Marshal hired people, whether relatives or strangers." His voice rose, thinned from distention so that she looked at him. His father could tell about people, yet had never relied on him so he must be no good. She did not figure that out at first, just thought confusedly of all the other men around his father that he disapproved of, like General Long Legs.

"That time we campaigned in the south I shared a room with Long Legs with just a curtain in between," he had said. "He called in three women and kept asking me, Have one? I just pulled the blanket over my head and pretended I was asleep."

Yet when they got to Shanghai he had played dominoes

with Long Legs and the other officers in a hotel room for over a week, night and day, with singsong girls trooping in and out getting bonuses. He beat them at their own games and preferred women that were out of their reach.

"There was the furor about the virgin that Long Legs had booked from a Shanghai singsong house, before leaving for the front. A virgin for good luck, like sacrificing to the flag. It turned out that he did not 'see red', so he wanted the madam's blood instead. Actually who dares cheat him? The girl must have had a secret lover and didn't dare tell the madam."

Still Long Legs was a man of the times like the Old Marshal while he himself was just the son, still untried after many battles. It was always seen to that he did not lose, or at least not lose face.

"I asked Yang and Ho about the plant and the railway. They had to go and look up the answers. This time I summoned them here and they were still evasive. I walked out of the room. A minute later the door opened and several officers shot them down," he whispered with a scared smile. "Ronald just heard. He must be thinking he's got into a robbers' den."

"Did you tell him why?"

"I told him about the head and tails too."

"No. What would people think?"

"He must have had a shock already seeing me so changed from the Peking days." He looked at himself in the mirror.

"You're thin. You haven't got over the trip back."

She readily saw his addiction as the rest of the household did, as an ailment that was a nuisance, though sometimes whispered about behind his back as an Achilles' heel. All he needed was the time to take the cure once the crisis of his father's death was over. Now the pressure was too great.

"Like those Peking opera singers," he said, "all the better-known ones have to take opium to keep up the strenuous life."

"And to appease their women admirers," one of his friends said slyly.

He laughed. "They do have this problem."

There was this group of young men who used to ride with him, the sons of officers or big landowners. He invited them to hunting parties at the new villa he built at the North Graves where the Manchu emperors were buried. Fourth Miss loved the North Graves, massive architecture in the Samarkand style that the Manchus had toned down, here at its simplest in a forest of tall pines. The villa was just a group of little red brick houses. She heard there were girls at those parties. It was a rumor because of his bad reputation, he said. Another time it was some of the men's wives dropping in for the gambling after the hunt. So-and-so's wife "keeps a close watch." They both thought it was very funny.

She was still called Fourth Miss in the house but he was now known as having two wives. Big Sister was glad of her narrow escape. If Fourth Miss was not with them already he would want a divorce now that his father was dead. As it was there was no question of raising the issue in a time like this. The three years' mourning also ruled out any celebrations, a thorny point originally. A simple feast was too much like taking a concubine. "Wait and see what the Old Marshal says," the Fifth Old Concubine had said. Now the problem was solved on all sides. A few quiet kowtows within the family sufficed. Her status was equal but not legal.

The three of them lived in the same courtyard, for convenience's sake Big Sister said, so he could get his clothes and things at once instead of sending for them. It was the time-honored stipulation of wives who did not want to be left out of the picture. She generally got her way. The other two were too content to make an issue of anything. The house was a copy of the Peking palace on a small scale. Across a wall and rock garden stood the three-storeyed office building with wood curlicues and a calligraphic board in the Old Marshal's own handwriting, "Heaven's law is men's heart." Another motto over the garden gate: "Walk the straight and narrow." They were surrounded by a flock of houses for the staff and guards, the Side Arms Company and Automobile Corps.

"When the new house is ready we'll ask Ronald to stay with us," he said. "Now he's more comfortable in the hotel."

"Has he got a family?" she said.

"He was married once."

"In America?"

"No, he's never been back all these years. They met in China. She's from his home state. He must have been homesick. But she left him because he was too engrossed in China."

She laughed. "Only foreign women would mind a thing like that."

"At least that's the story. But he's known as a regular Confucius. Secretary Sung was comparing him to Confucius traveling through all the kingdoms looking for a ruler that would practise his teachings. To keep him from going south last year Old Chow specially created the Bureau of Statistics for him so he could collect figures to his heart's content. Americans believe in them. He got a thousand a month to run it. Old Chow said, 'That fool Ronald, the thousand was for him, I never expected him to hire a staff and pay out salaries.' What's more he paid them out of his own pocket after Peking fell. Nanking promised him to keep the bureau going but never paid him back in the end."

She loved to hear them talk. It gave her a feeling she had never had before, of sitting in a high pavilion open to the sun and wind looking clear across the plains to the Yellow River. It was all there before her even though muddied by all the unfamiliar proper names made still more confusing by Ronald's mispronunciations. He also said some incredible things, like he himself had paid for demonstrators against the Twenty-one Demands. In her year at college she had learned that the protest march was a milestone in the students' movement and national awakening. But she believed him, and at the same time felt a little dubious and affronted by the way everybody was made out to be such fools, Sun Yatsun for instance:

"A reporter asked, 'Are you a socialist, Dr. Sun?' He turned to me saying, 'Am I?' I said, 'You're everything a Nationalist has to be.' "

"So the good doctor is finally reburied in style, beside the Ming emperors," the Young Marshal said.

"In the most grandiose sugar cake. Over ten thousand people petitioned against having their houses torn down to build the highway across town just to get the casket to the mountain."

"How is it the body is not on display after all the trouble of preserving it?"

"They don't want to be copycat to Lenin now that they broke with the Communists."

"What do you think of the new brother-in-law and successor? He's got the ancestral tablet in both hands now."

She picked up her ears. That was the man who married his old love.

"I don't really know him, except through his brothers-in-law."

"Theirs is government by brothers-in-law."

"Was he really legally divorced?" The one time she spoke up she modestly addressed her question to the Young Marshal. They left her out of the conversation in the Oriental way with ladies.

"Yes," Ronald answered.

"Country wives are easy to handle," said the Young

Marshal.

"In a case like this you can't just tuck a wife away in the country. And he'd gone as far as to turn Christian."

"What's this about his son denouncing him?"

"That's the son he sent to Russia in his Russian period. The Russians always have sons denouncing their fathers. The boy is a Youth Pioneer. A Chinese Communist underground publication printed his open letter to his mother, accusing his father of betraying the revolution."

"And kicking his mother downstairs for asking him not to go to singsong houses," the Young Marshal chortled.

"That was when he was in business in Shanghai."

"Was that the wife he divorced?" she asked. She had seen the engagement photograph of Miss Soo-hoo and him, she round-shouldered in ruffled chiffon, with smiling eyes on a rather large soft face under marcelled waves, he standing behind her in uniform, tall, thin and clean-cut. Did she love him? She got what she was looking for, the ruler of China. And she was his own choice instead of the wife his family had foisted on him. There was a great difference there.

"Is it true he made a million on the stock exchange?"

"He lost it in the crash."

"Enough to make a man join the revolution."

"He'd joined early, in army school. But after the Nationalist defeat in Shanghai many went underground, some worked on the Exchange and met in singsong houses. He seemed to have merged into the scene rather well, stayed around for ten years."

"He's good at about-facing."

"He rode a dangerous current to the top. Trouble is nothing has changed. All the old forces gathering, more civil wars. Meanwhile Nanking doesn't do a thing that makes any difference. I stayed long enough to see they're time-wasters. Now I call them Nationa-lusts."

"Yes, same old China. If only we can kill off several million people. Then maybe we can get something done."

"That's the Bolshevik method."

"As long as it works."

"I don't know about that. The Great Experiment has been on for nearly ten years now and they're still famished. Militarily Russia is the one country nobody is afraid of."

"Here at least it got us back the foreign settlements in Hankow."

"They're the least of your worries. Get enough peace and order in the rest of the country and you'll attract as much investment. You don't even use the same money in all the provinces."

"If only we can hand over the country to some reliable foreign power for twenty-five years."

"Unfortunately that can't be arranged."

"Most of my countrymen will be angry at me for saying this, but they haven't tried to get things done, or never had a chance to try."

"I can see how you got known as a radical."

"Only because I'm my father's son and could speak more freely."

"I'm glad you're not of the prevailing view blaming everything on foreigners and unequal treaties. Actually China needs more foreign capital, more boards of control, not less. I say this although I fought the Consortium twice just as a newspaperman." He launched into the story of how he had tricked them out of the land tax marked down as security.

"Ronald talks a lot but he knows how to keep his mouth shut," he told her more than a year later. "He knew about Yang and Ho. They'd sent somebody to see him in Shanghai offering him two thousand pounds to go to London and negotiate a fifteen million pound loan to develop Manchuria. He said it couldn't be done. When he first came here he spoke to those two about it but they quickly changed the subject. He thought that was odd and suspected they wanted the money for a coup. It would have meant a lot to me if he'd told me this after they were executed. But he said nothing. That was real character. No matter who comes to him for advice it's confidential."

"Then how did you get to know?"

"He just mentioned it, now that we really know each other."

Ronald persuaded him to get rid of the drug habit and took charge of his diet, introducing some of his own favorite health foods. He could argue for hours about the relative merits of agar-agar and bran. He made him cut out the parties, played golf and swam and fished with him, took him on long hikes to tire him out completely. There were worries about assassination on country lanes. The Japanese Kwantung Army officers had been yelling around ever since he recognized Nanking as the central government, "Punish Chan Shu-tan, he betrayed us."

She was happy to see the two go off like boy scouts. But his health got so bad the doctor advised complete rest and seclusion for at least a month.

"The rumors will have me dead," he said at once. "There will be uprisings, an opening for the Japanese."

He went back to the drug. "I'll be the first to go for the cure when we have the hospital for it."

There were no funds for the hospital after building the university and a modern port. Settlers poured in from north and central China where there had been wars. The latest was the biggest yet, both sides had half a million men in the field. Three hundred thousand died. Both Nanking and the Christian General and his ally "the king of Shansi" pressed the Young Marshal to join them. He took the stand against civil wars but they kept at him.

She heard Ronald say at lunch, strangely upset, "So far nobody has touched it. The one thing that represents Chinese unity as a nation."

"The Chinese just see it as part of the unequal treaties," he said.

"If they seized the Customs on the pretext of customs autonomy, why install an Englishman as commissioner? Exchange one Englishman for another, that's what I don't understand."

"Old Yin has been too cooped up in Shansi. No experience in foreign affairs."

"And to have Gravesend-Kemp of all people."

"He's unscrupulous enough. And a well-known writer."

"That makes it all right for him to do anything out here among the comic opera war lords. It's fun, and there may be a book in it."

They went to play golf. The next she heard was, "We're going in."

She thought it was agreed that he should stay out as long as possible.

"Only on condition that the Nationalists clean house and open up the government," Ronald had said. "And not just promises."

She did not want him to go to war and so was familiar with all the arguments against it—leaving Manchuria half empty, Japan would move in. Manchuria was more industrialized than any other part of China. The Nationalist representative had been all agog when he was taken over the munitions plant and it took three hours to drive him over the lot. The country was so big and potentially rich it would be more profitable to develop it than join in civil wars. In the final accounting the Old Marshal's wars had cost more than he got out of it.

"So you have your isolationists too," Ronald had said.

"Why does Ronald hate that Englishman so much?" she

asked.

"Oh, Gravesend-Kemp. He's the kind of foreigner in China who's out for all he can get, and Ronald himself has always been scrupulous about money."

"They've known each other a long time?" Perhaps wives are prone to suspect their husband's best friend of using him. She felt uneasy and guilty.

"In Peking. Gravesend-Kemp wrote many books on China, said to be brilliant. Ronald also writes."

" 'Literary men are contemptuous of each other; it has been so since ancient times,' "she quoted laughing.

"And when was that said?"

"I don't know. About fifteen hundred years ago."

The coming test hung heavy over them. He was to enter what the newspapers called the Great War of the Central Plains and the Battle over the Nation. Japan was behind the other side. She never wanted to put him to any tests because they were unfair. The old saying was Do not judge a hero by success or defeat.

He went inside the Pass and sent for her as promised, along with Big Sister, as soon as he had found a house in Peking, avoiding the Marshal's House and any identification with the old regime. This time the Manchurians had come as the army of peace. The war was over the minute he appeared over the border.

His favorite story of the campaign was about Gravesend-Kemp.

"He wrote me at headquarters. Offered me two million in cash and a million a month if I would keep the Customs independent. I asked him to come and see me.

" 'Why did you do that?' Ronald said.

" 'I want to see an Englishman lose face.'

" 'Be careful. People will take it that you just didn't come to terms.'

" 'You'll be there as witness.'

" 'I don't know. He'd assume that you're interested. If you do work out something you'd have gained a friend and lost another. Because I'll have to leave you.' "

Ronald had threatened this before. He had happened to run into an old acquaintance in Mukden, an English baronet in the Indian civil service and then in the legation.

"What are you doing here?" Ronald asked.

"The Young Marshal asked me to be his advisor."

The Young Marshal announced at dinner at home, "Ronald

threw down the gauze hat," the hat of office. "Jealous as a woman."

"Jealous as a woman indeed," Big Sister said. "Put out your hand and feel your own conscience."

"So Gravesend-Kemp came to headquarters. 'You simply must reappoint me,' he said.

"I said Why?

" 'Because of the money we can make together.'

" 'By robbing the Customs.'

" 'I wouldn't know what to do if you won't help me.'

" 'Ask Yin Shih-san.'

" 'He's run away.'

" 'Then you run away.'

" 'Will you give me a week?'

" 'Why?'

" 'I have to take care of my staff.'

" 'Give you a week to rob the Customs! I'll give you one day to hand it back to the proper authorities.'

"He hurried off. Two days later one of his employees shot him for the loot. Heaven knows it's difficult for a foreigner to get himself killed in China. Probably the first civilian since the Boxers. And for once England didn't send gunboats."

In those first hazy days of incredulous triumph the story was the one thing that made it real for her. Gravesend-Kemp was practically the only casualty of the war. The three hundred thousand anonymous dead was before he got in. Yin of Shansi still had the province to himself after temporary asylum in Dairen. The Christian General had retired with his wife and choice troops up a scenic mountain in Shantung. Nanking was satisfied to leave it at that. Keeping their names on the wanted list throughout the country was enough punishment. But for the death of the Englishman it was as baffling and dreamlike as a leaky pillow fight, punching into clouds of fluff. She got the impression that the interview at headquarters was the first high point of his life. He had finally proved himself and before Ronald who was the world.

"One odd thing," Ronald said, "in his first book you can see what impressed him most in the Boxers Rebellion was the looting. To think he'd die of it after thirty years."

" 'Peking Indiscreet'," she said.

"Yes. It's a good first-hand account. You can see him drooling."

"He also has a short story called 'Loot'."

"Oh? What's it about?"

"It's the same story."

"The British and Indians and Cossacks looting the palace?"

"Yes, he rewrote that into a short story eight years later."

"I'll be damned."

"I never knew you read him," the Young Marshal said happily.

"I got curious. You were talking about him."

He liked to show her off to Ronald but she generally kept quiet. Ronald was careful with her and was correct in paying her less attention than if she was an unmarried girl of the house. He loved to tease young girls, English-speaking ones perforce. But when a man had two wives it was safer to assume that they were old-fashioned, no matter how modern they seemed.

"He justified it all along," Ronald said. "They were Drake's pirates looting from the looters. The Manchu themselves had got it from the Ming emperors. As to the foreign-manned customs, theirs is the fruit of imperialist exploitation, although this may sound too Bolshie for him."

"So he was just doing what he had always believed in," the Young Marshal said.

"Writers are not supposed to. Barking dogs you know."

He was made Deputy Commander-in-chief of the Armed

Forces of China and flew to Nanking with Ronald to attend the National Assembly. Rumors said he would never come back. Nanking would hold him or his father's old officers would take over Manchuria. He came back in two months. He had put an end to the war lords' era. The next time his wives went with him in their private plane. It was the twentieth century at last, thirty years late and he with two wives but he got in. China was in.

图书在版编目（CIP）数据

少帅／张爱玲著；郑远涛译 .—北京：北京十月
文艺出版社，2015.9
ISBN 978-7-5302-1469-5

Ⅰ.①少… Ⅱ.①张…②郑… Ⅲ.①长篇小说－中
国－现代 Ⅳ.①I246.5

中国版本图书馆CIP数据核字（2015）第043001号

著作权合同登记号 图字：01-2015-2149

本书由张爱玲著作权所有人宋以朗先生和其独家版权代理皇冠文化集团授
权，仅限于中国大陆地区销售，不得售至台、港、澳地区，及新、马、美、
加等任何海外地区。

责任编辑 李成强
特邀编辑 林妮娜 赵丽苗
装帧设计 朱 琳
内文制作 王春雪
责任印制 李远林 李海坡 史广宜

少帅
SHAOSHUAI

张爱玲 著 郑远涛 译

出　　版　北京出版集团公司　　　北京十月文艺出版社
　　　　　北京北三环中路6号　　　邮编 100120
发　　行　新经典发行有限公司
　　　　　电话 (010)68423599　　　邮箱 editor@readinglife.com
经　　销　新华书店
印　　刷　北京国彩印刷有限公司
开　　本　850 毫米×1168 毫米 1/32
印　　张　6.75
字　　数　110 千
版　　次　2015 年 9 月第 1 版
印　　次　2015 年 11 月第 4 次印刷
书　　号　ISBN 978-7-5302-1469-5
定　　价　39.50 元
质量监督电话 010-58572393